It was after dark by the time we got to the small town of Draper's Heights. The lights of the houses and stores lining the main streets looked friendly and inviting, but Uncle Walker drove right on through to the outskirts. He turned off onto a paved drive that wound upward through tangles of unkempt shrubbery. The track was so narrow that branches clawed at the car as our headlights slashed the darkness.

At last the driveway widened and the hill flattened out. An angular shape blacker than the sky squatted among the trees, as though its very presence drained the darkness from the night. An unseen hand flicked on an entrance light, but the square of butter yellow falling over the stone steps did little to push back the inky blackness.

"Here we are," my uncle announced. "Welcome to Blackbird Keep."

Dear Readers:

Thank you for your unflagging interest in First Love From Silhouette. Your many helpful letters have shown us that you have appreciated growing and stretching with us, and that you demand more from your reading than happy endings and conventional love stories. In the months to come we will make sure that our stories go on providing the variety you have come to expect from us. We think you will enjoy our unusual plot twists and unpredictable characters who will surprise and delight you without straying too far from the concerns that are very much part of all our daily lives.

We hope you will continue to share with us your ideas about how to keep our books your very First Loves. We depend on you to keep us on our toes!

Nancy Jackson
Senior Editor
FIRST LOVE FROM SILHOUETTE

BLACKBIRD KEEP
Candice Ransom

First Love from Silhouette

Published by Silhouette Books New York

America's Publisher of Contemporary Romance

For the Marva Writer's Workshop

SILHOUETTE BOOKS
300 E. 42nd St., New York, N.Y. 10017

ISBN: 0-373-06175-7

First Silhouette Books printing February 1986

America's Publisher of Contemporary Romance

Printed in the U.S.A.

RL 6.4, IL Age 11 and up

CANDICE RANSOM was born in Washington, D.C., and brought up in Centreville, Virginia, where she still lives with her husband and a bossy black cat. She began her first book in second grade and has been writing off and on ever since. She particularly enjoys writing about the past; even her mysteries have a touch of nostalgia. Old carousels, turn-of-the-century picture books, antique toys and miniatures often appear in the background of her stories.

Chapter One

From the very first the jester knew everything. The moment I stepped through the front door of Blackbird Keep, our eyes met—only the jester's were painted on wood and mine probably looked frightened.

"Holly, you see my pride and joy," Uncle Walker said, coming in behind me with my suitcase. "I collect old toys, you know. This jester was quite a find. It was carved by Maxfield Parrish when he was only nineteen," he added reverently, glancing at me to see if I was suitably impressed.

I didn't know Maxfield Parrish from Adam, but the doll grabbed my attention immediately. It wasn't like anything I had ever seen before, and certainly not in someone's hallway.

The jester's head was carved from wood, with slit eyes and a mouth that showed small even teeth. Its long jaw ended in a pointed chin. Chipped yellow paint lacquered the face, while rosy color highlighted the cheekbones and nose. A black satin hood covered its head, with petals of pink, yellow and black satin framing the wicked little face. Golden bells bobbled from the satin flaps.

Fastened onto a dowel, the doll's head protruded from a brass umbrella stand in the shape of an elephant's leg. I guessed it to be very old—the satin cap was mended in several places and the paint on the stick was scratched and faded. I could picture a harlequin-garbed fool capering before an amused Henry VIII, waving the jester, his own likeness, to make the king laugh.

Not notice the jester? In this dreary, stone-flagged entryway, lit only by wall sconces that cast a weird, flickering light, how could I miss such a curious thing?

The worst part, I decided, shifting my crutches to a more comfortable position, was that the jester seemed to know everything about me—including fragments of my past that remained a mystery even to me. The parted red lips appeared ready to speak; the narrow eyes stared woodenly into mine, mocking me. If a magician suddenly granted it the power of speech, I know the jester would grin menacingly and say in a creaking voice, "You don't belong here, Holly Highsmith. Go away."

And it would be absolutely right. I did not belong at Blackbird Keep.

They say bad luck comes in bunches of three. Normally I'm not a superstitious person, but the month before school let out for the summer, it was as though the witches in *Macbeth* had brewed a big batch of trouble, tripling their recipe.

It began with my mother's bombshell announcement, which she dropped one morning shortly before school ended.

I was gloomy enough that May morning, my spirits thoroughly dampened by the past two weeks of rain and the fact that Tony Leotta had somehow overlooked asking me to the sophomore Spring Fling. I had counted on being at that dance, but Saturday night came and went and my white pumps were still collecting dust on my closet floor. Shelby, who had gone with Lane Browning, had dutifully called me Sunday, like the reliable best friend she was, to report that Tony had not shown up with someone else, as I had feared. Yet that did little to comfort me.

Winds blew miserable gusts of soggy leaves across our patio, which stuck to the glass doors like leeches. Spring seemed as far away as Christmas. As I poured myself a glass of orange juice, thinking longingly of white sand beaches and palm trees lazily waving against a sunny sky, Mom came into the kitchen.

"I went over our finances last night," she proclaimed, her coffee cup clinking against the saucer—a sure sign she was agitated. "Things don't look good, Holly. Not at all."

I should have known what was coming next. Whenever Mom made that statement, it usually meant another cutback at the Highsmith household. I steeled myself to sacrifice the fashion magazines I was addicted to or for packing lunches five days a week instead of three.

"What is it now?" I asked half-jokingly, not really anticipating the worst. "Do we have to make our own mustard? I'll get out the old mortar and pestle and start grinding the seeds. Never let it be said I didn't do my fair share."

If we couldn't laugh about our money troubles once in a while, we would have been declared certifiable years ago. To be truthful, there was nothing funny about the way we had to watch every penny. Worrying about money loomed ever present in our lives, like a big black balloon that followed us everywhere. Or the Grim Reaper, depending on how you viewed things.

Mom bluntly ignored my feeble attempt at levity. "I wish we could solve this by making our own mustard. I have to ax our vacation, Holly. We just can't swing three weeks in Florida. I'll write to the real-estate man and see if we can get our deposit back."

"Not our trip!" I wailed. "We haven't been anywhere in *years*. Mom, you *promised*." I was prepared to make my own prom dress out of discarded paper towels and carry sandwiches until I was drawing Social Security...*anything* but give up that vacation.

"I'm sorry, Holly. If we were independently wealthy..."

If we were independently wealthy we wouldn't be having this discussion. I scrambled for a solution. "Okay, we don't have to spend three weeks there. How about two weeks?"

She shook her head resolutely.

"One week?" How could a person shake her head that way and not jar her brains loose? "A long weekend?"

"It's not just the time there," Mom explained. "Plane fare from Indiana to Florida is the biggest money-eater. More than the hotel. I missed the opportunity to get one of those super-saver deals airlines offer from time to time because we never had the ready cash."

"I don't suppose we can afford the train?" Desperation was making me resort to the ridiculous. "How about hitchhiking and staying at the Y?"

Mom sighed. "Holly—"

"All right. No Florida. No beaches. No fantastic sun." I threw myself across the table, a posture of grief that would have made the most devout Hindu widow envious. "I guess I'll spend an afternoon at the travel agency, drooling over brochures and posters. That'll be my vacation. I sure hope we don't have to write an essay about our summer in English class next fall. Mine will be so dull, the teacher will probably give me an F for boring her to death." Of course, I would hardly be given such an infantile assignment in my junior year of high school, but I had to take my disappointment out on somebody.

When I saw hurt film over my mother's violet eyes, I regretted dumping on her. It wasn't her fault we were always broke.

"You don't know how sorry I am, knowing we have to suffer another long, hot summer in this town," she said. "But numbers don't lie. The money I set aside for the trip just dribbled away. Pipkin had to go to the vet twice—"

From his place under the table, my golden retriever guiltily swished his plumed tail at the mention of his name, as if embarrassed that his respiratory infection had cost us our R and R. I reached down and patted his head to let him know it was okay.

Mom continued her dismal litany. "The car needed a new battery... I had that root canal... the furnace croaked—"

"You don't have to go on. I get the picture." I hid my eyes with my hands, as if the prospect of spending the whole summer here in Miller's Forks was too terrible to face.

"It all adds up, Holly. The worst part is we have no fallback fund, now that our vacation money is gone. I was hoping to replenish it with our tax refund, but that went, too. That's the trouble with robbing Peter to pay Paul."

Living hand to mouth, she meant.

Life had been hard after my father's death. Even though he passed away nearly ten years ago, shortly before my sixth birthday, my mother still struggled to keep the wolves from the door. Her position at the Indiana National Bank branch just outside of Miller's Forks enabled us to maintain the modest bungalow Daddy had purchased, which was located in the last of the nice old residential neighborhoods.

"No matter what," Mom would tell me, even when I was too young to know what a mortgage was, "we have to hang onto the house. Your father worked very hard to get it and nobody is going to take it away from us."

We hung onto the house.

But during the past few years we really felt the pinch of an ever-tightening economy. At first it was only little luxuries we gave up. Our Friday nights out—reserved as our special weekly breathers—were downgraded from dinner at Evan's Farm Inn, one of the best restaurants in town, to the McDonald's in nearby Halloway, to tuna casserole at home. Leftover tuna casserole, at that. And the toll of this past winter, with one illness or disaster on the heels of another, showed in the deep worry lines bracketing my mother's mouth like parentheses.

Which was one reason I had pinned all my hopes on a trip to Florida. Three weeks on a sunny beach was just what we needed. Three weeks away from Miller's Forks, away from incessant hassles. I knew a vacation wouldn't make our hardships vanish, but at least Mom would get a break.

"I wish I could help," I said wistfully.

"School will be out soon. Mrs. Barton promised you lots of baby-sitting jobs."

I frowned. "Couldn't I get a real job this summer?" I had been taking Mrs. Barton's monsters to the pool for the past three years. Of course, without David and Deirdre, who tried to drown each other every chance they got, my tootsies wouldn't touch a drop of chlorinated water the whole summer. Membership to the community pool was an extravagance beyond even casual consideration.

"We've been over this before, Holly. I don't want you to get a job yet, no matter how much we need money. You have the rest of your life to work. I want you to do your best in school, without juggling homework and a counter job at Sweeney's."

She had a point. A lot of kids I knew skimped on their school assignments or were tired in class because they worked so late. And with my schedule I had to be on my toes every minute. This year I was carrying a full academic load plus three business courses. "Just in case you won't be able to go to college right away," Mom had told me last year when we went over the list of classes offered. "If we don't have the money and you can't get a scholarship, at least you can go to work as a secretary."

Secretarial work didn't exactly thrill me, but I knew Mom's anxiety stemmed from having single motherhood thrust upon her so suddenly. College seemed light years away, especially since I hadn't the faintest notion what I wanted to do with my life. I wish I could be like my friend Shelby. Since third grade she had resolved to be a forest ranger. Impatient to turn her dream into reality, she was already sending out applications to the state parks, even though graduation was two years away.

"I'm sorry," Mom said again. "I know how much you counted on getting away."

I went over and put an arm around her shoulder. "Don't give it another thought. We'll get along. Maybe I'll win the lottery and our biggest problem will be deciding whether to take the Concorde to Paris or the *QE II* to London."

That made her smile. "Just you and me, kid."

Wasn't that the way it had always been? Just my mother and me against the world? And I could always meet a boy even cuter than Tony Leotta at the pool.

I had just about resigned myself to another hopeless summer here in town, when the second bad thing happened.

Shelby asked me to go horseback riding with her the last Saturday before school ended. She had been taking lessons for months, but this was only my fourth time on a horse. I was sitting in the saddle as if it were a rocking chair, the reins slack, when Peppermint suddenly reared. I fell backward, one foot twisting in the stirrup, and was dangling in this painful position as I heard a sickening snap.

My leg was fractured in two places. I spent one miserable afternoon at St. Luke's Hospital, my left leg encased in a thick cast from knee to heel, dreams of an interesting summer dashed once and for all. Even if I had won the lottery, I could scarcely go clumping aboard the *QE II* like this.

I was excused from the last unproductive days of school—which wasn't so bad. But I also missed the end-of-the-year parties, which Tony Leotta escorted Susan Watson to—which was terrible. With my shoulder-length brown hair, it was hard enough to compete with Susan's auburn mane, but a broken leg at a dance was the kiss of death.

I was imprisoned on our side porch, sentenced to a grim existence of crossword puzzles and soap operas, when the third bad thing arrived disguised as something wonderful.

Mom came home from work early one afternoon, laden with an order of takeout chicken, papers blooming from her handbag.

I sat up at the sight of the red-and-white-striped bucket, a rare treat. "Mom?"

"Holly, it's the strangest thing!" Her purplish blue eyes, so different from the tea-colored eyes I'd inherited from Daddy, glowed with a light I hadn't seen in ages. She set the bucket on the round patio table.

"Tell me!" The puzzle book slid to the concrete floor as I straightened my leg on the glider cushion. I had had my cast replaced once and my doctor said my leg was "knitting nicely."

"You don't want to eat first?" She lifted the lid from the bucket, tantalizing me with the aroma of the Colonel's finest.

"Mo-om!"

"All right." She replaced the lid. "I'll tell you. This has been the most astonishing day. First Mr. Pinkney calls me in his office. You'll never guess, Holly—the bank has chosen me for an extensive management-training course. Me! Ms. Highsmith, I should say." She rolled her eyes in a parody of a big-time executive.

"A course? You mean, like school?"

She nodded. "Mr. Pinkney is grooming me to be a manager. Do you realize what this means? A promotion—more money. And a more secure position."

"That's great, Mom. When do you start?"

"Next week. The thing is, the training institute is in Olive Branch, Mississippi."

"Where?" A name that weird should have been in my crossword puzzle. Twenty-four down: a peaceful town in a Southern state famous for its river.

"I know. I've never heard of it, either. The course is ten weeks. I have to take it, Holly. A chance like this is too good to pass up."

"That's okay, Mom. I'll get a vacation, after all. Even if it is in—what was the name of that place again?"

"Olive Branch. But you can't go. The course is very intensive—the institute frowns on families going along...that's probably why they have the school in such a remote place. Fewer distractions."

So now I'm a distraction. A frumpy distraction with a broken leg and no boyfriend. Things were getting worse by the second. "What am I supposed to do? Sit here all by myself all summer?" The heavy cast and the leaden news made me whiny. Everybody in the entire world was going away and here I sat, weighted down with ten pounds of plaster and the knowledge that I was, at least in the eyes of training institutes, a liability.

"That's the really strange part." Mom plucked an envelope from her purse. "This came in today's mail."

I couldn't make out the name in the left-hand corner, but I could see our address had been written in raven-black ink, the letters spiky and decisive, yet slightly scratchy and old-fashioned, as though penned with a quill. "Who's it from?"

Mom took a deep breath. "Your Uncle Walker. Arthur's brother."

My father's brother! Since Dad's death ten years ago, we hadn't heard a syllable from Walker Highsmith. I stared at the envelope, then at my mother.

Dad's side of the family was the world's best-kept secret, outside of the combination to the vault at Fort Knox. I vaguely recalled some disagreement between Dad and my grandfather that I never understood. When my father died, only Uncle Walker came to the funeral, because by then Grandfather Highsmith was too sick. Or so he claimed. Maybe it was true, because my grandfather died about five years ago. I remember Mom getting the phone call from Uncle Walker, who was another odd duck. The whole family seemed bizarre, what was left of it.

As if reading my thoughts, Mom said, "Walker was the only one of your father's brothers who remained on friendly terms with your grandfather after the big blowup."

"What big blowup? And what other brothers? I didn't know Daddy had any besides Uncle Walker."

"One," Mom replied. "His name is Merton. There were three Highsmith boys: Walker, Merton and your father."

Three Highsmith boys—just like the three princes in a fairy tale.

"I've never heard of Merton." I mulled over the name. I just gained an uncle I never knew I had. It was a peculiar feeling, as though someone had control of my past, which they would dole out to me in bits and pieces whenever they chose. I didn't like it.

Mom must have sensed what I was thinking. "I know, Holly. It's hard. For years I didn't know anything, either. I'll tell you what I know. Seth Highsmith—your grandfather—was quite well off. He'd made a fortune in Europe between the wars. Doing what, I'm not sure. He bought a wonderful old house in Delaware for his bride. But after his wife died—that was your grandmother—he became stern, even hateful. Arthur and his brothers grew up in a loveless home. Walker left home first to go away to school—Oxford. When he graduated, he brought back an English wife. They have one child. A daughter, about your age."

"What about Daddy?" I pressed. I had the feeling Mom wasn't anxious to tell the next part. "How come he didn't get along with his father?"

She twisted a strand of honey-colored hair, stalling. "Apparently Arthur and Mert fell in love with a girl in the village. They argued constantly, got into fights. Around that same time, some irreplaceable heirloom disappeared. Seth accused Arthur of giving it to the girl. There was another blowup, this time between your father and your grandfather. I don't know what happened exactly—your father never said—but he left shortly after that and never went back."

Banished from the kingdom, I thought. "What happened to the other brother? Merton?"

"He left, too. Walker wrote to Arthur a few times, sent a card once in a while. He thought Mert was married and living in Wisconsin."

"And the girl? The one they both liked? What became of her?"

"Nothing, I guess." A frown marred my mother's lovely features. Was she jealous because Daddy had once loved someone else? "Anyway, it was over a long time ago."

Yes, it was all a long time ago. But far from over, I was to learn.

"What does Uncle Walker say in his letter?" I asked with a funny clutch in my throat. "He hasn't written in all these years . . . what can he possibly want now?"

Mom drew a deep, relieved breath. "That's the strange part, Holly. The way everything fell into place in one remarkable day. You see, when Mr. Pinkney offered me the school, my first thought was of you, naturally. I couldn't take you and you couldn't stay here alone."

"I could stay with Shelby," I put in. "For a while, anyway." Shelby's family went to their cabin in the Berkshires every July and August.

Mom went on as if I hadn't spoken. "And then I open the mailbox and there between the bill from Peeble's and my Literary Guild selection was the answer to our problem." She indicated the letter lying on the table. "You can read it, if you like. Uncle Walker wants you to come stay with them this summer. He's even offered to pay your air fare."

I shifted my leg again. "Me? He wants me to visit? Why? I don't even know him."

My mother tapped the envelope with one fingernail. "Walker doesn't come right out and admit it, but I think he's having trouble with his daughter."

"What does his bratty kid have to do with me?" I didn't like the sound of this. "What am I supposed to do?"

"Nothing. Just…be there. I gather Alexandra doesn't have many friends. I guess Walker thinks you might—be a good influence on her."

I stared at her. "How can he think that? He doesn't know anything about me."

"Sometimes people turn to their families, Holly."

"Oh, really? What about us? Where was he all those years after Daddy died? He remembers us when it's convenient for him." I slumped back, blowing my bangs upward in a gesture of disgust.

"If you don't want to go," Mom said quietly, "I understand. We can make other arrangements."

"What other arrangements?" I asked skeptically. "I know how important this school is to you. The problem is, we've run out of relatives."

"There's always my cousin Bobby in Stamford," she suggested archly.

"The one with the Lawnmower Hall of Fame in his garage? No, thanks."

My mother was an only child, of parents who were also only children and who had died long before I was born. Cousin Bobby was actually a second or third cousin—I could never remember which. We went to visit his wife and him the summer after Daddy died, at their invitation. The only part of the visit that stood out in my memory was Cousin Bobby's fetish for lawnmowers. He had every kind known to man, shrined in a grease-spotty, gasoline-smelling garage. Riding mowers, push mowers, power mowers that ran on electricity. You name it and he had it.

I looked over at Mom. "You aren't seriously considering sending me to stay with old Lawn Boy, now are you?"

We both knew the answer to that.

The letter lay between us on the table like a royal summons. Even though I hadn't read a word, I could feel the power within that envelope. I wanted to go to Delaware about as much as I wanted a spinal tap. Yet I sensed a spell at work here. I had no choice in the matter at all.

Getting off the plane with crutches was an experience not to be missed. I looked around the airport, unable to believe I was actually in Wilmington and wondering how I would know my father's eldest brother. My uncle found me first. I suppose I wasn't hard to identify, since I was the only fifteen-year-old girl on crutches.

"I'm Walker Highsmith," said the tall, sandy-haired man, singling me out from the confused knot of disembarking passengers. "It's been a while, but we met once."

"At my father's funeral," I replied flatly. "Ten years ago." I wanted to trigger a flash of guilt.

But he merely blinked and said, "Yes, I guess it has been that long. You haven't met my wife, Gray."

A slender willowy woman with silver hair and limpid hazel eyes came forward, one slim hand extended.

I thought the unusual names suited them both. Uncle Walker seemed very efficient and brisk as he collected my luggage, capable of walking to the ends of the earth if he had to. My Aunt Gray had a vague, wispy air about her. She smiled gently at me. I wondered why their daughter—the one I was supposed to help—didn't come, too.

As it turned out, the house my father left so long ago, where my uncle lived now, had the strangest name of all.

Blackbird Keep.

"Originally the house was called Belleview, or something equally lackluster," Walker said. "But my father changed the name when he began studying birds."

My grandfather studied birds? The ogre who drove away two of his three sons was a bird-watcher? It didn't fit.

It was after dark when we arrived in the small town of Draper's Heights. The lights of the houses and stores lining the main street seemed friendly and inviting, but Uncle Walker drove right on through to the outskirts. He turned off onto a paved drive that wound upward through tangles of unkempt shrubbery. The track was so narrow, branches clawed at the car. The beam of our headlights sliced through the darkness, sometimes capturing pinpoints of red that blinked once, then vanished.

"Rabbits," Uncle Walker explained.

At last the driveway widened as the hill flattened out. An angular shape blacker than the sky squatted among the trees, as though its very presence siphoned the darkness from the night. An unseen hand flicked on an entrance light, but the square of butter yellow falling over stone steps did little to push back the inky blackness.

"Here we are," my uncle announced. "Blackbird Keep. Your grandfather would be proud that Arthur's daughter was returning to the house he loved and cherished. He'd be the first to welcome you."

I had my doubts. Hobbling into the hallway on my crutches, I was certain Blackbird Keep could never present anything but a sinister face, at least to me. Then I saw the jester leering at me from the umbrella stand, and in that instant, I knew that coming here was a big mistake.

Chapter Two

We all stood awkwardly in the hallway. I was starting to worry that I hadn't acted reverent enough over Uncle Walker's prized possession by swooning or something, when he said, "As long as you're interested, Holly, I'll show you my toy room."

Toy room? A grown man who still kept toys? Curiouser and curiouser.

Aunt Gray rushed to my rescue. "Walker, dear," she said in a voice that reminded me of cool water running over smooth round stones, "Holly can see your collection in the morning. I'm sure she must be exhausted. The flight and then the long drive from Wilmington..."

I *was* tired. Lugging the cast around wore me out—it was like carrying a ten-pound sack of cat litter everywhere I went—and I still had not gotten used to the crutches. They were aluminum, with pads on the crosspieces, but the hollows under my arms were sore and tender. It probably wasn't all that late, nine or so, yet I felt as if I'd mushed a dogsled team over a thousand miles of uncharted ice.

"I'd really like to see your—uh, toy room, Uncle Walker—" I tried to sound convincing "—but I'm kind of wiped out."

Uncle Walker waved away my excuses. "Nonsense. It won't take a second. You should be introduced to my collection at night. In the daytime…well, you'll see what I mean. This way, please. Gray, are you coming?" This last was addressed to my aunt, who shrank beside me, as if she'd rather do anything than follow her husband into his toy room.

My impressions of these people were changing by the minute, as though they were shapeshifters altering their identities right before my eyes. Walker had gone from my crisp, efficient uncle at the airport, to an eccentric who collected toys, to this stern stranger who seemed used to having his authority unquestioned. Aunt Gray had transformed from the soft-spoken woman I first saw in the airport to a pale, clinging shadow, like a morning-glory vine fading in harsh, noonday sun. Was she afraid of her husband?

Uncle Walker was already leading the way down the dim hallway. Gray smiled weakly at me and gestured, as if to say, "After you." My underarm muscles were screaming in protest, but I leaned on my crutches and hobbled after my uncle with a resigned sigh.

He stopped at a doorway on the right. I could see the passageway continuing beyond this door at some length—Blackbird Keep was big enough to qualify as a mansion.

"A friend of mine who does stained glass made me this window," Uncle Walker was saying. The heavy carved door was inset with a leaded glass rectangle that spelled out Toy Shop. Walker fished a ring of keys from his pocket. "Are you ready?"

"Walker, for heaven's sake," Gray spoke up. "The child is practically asleep on her feet. Don't drag this out all night."

I nodded at him, ready as I'd ever be to see a grown man's collection of fire engines and trains. When my uncle unlocked the door and pushed it inward, I realized then why the jester was grinning at me from the umbrella stand in the hall.

The joke was clearly on me.

There wasn't one single toy fire engine, or one choo-choo train tooting and huffing through a homemade village. Nothing that innocuous.

The ceiling-high shelves on three sides were laden with faces, all wearing gremlin smiles of self-satisfaction, as if they'd known I was coming. Hundreds of eyes focused on me as I crabbed into the room. I caught my breath in one quick gasp and dropped one of my crutches, which clattered to the stone floor. While my uncle hurried to pick it up, I noticed the eyes were mostly glass and that the faces were frozen into those peculiar expressions.

Dolls of every description sat shoulder to shoulder, legs dangling over the shelves. None of your Barbies or Cabbage Patch Kids here. They were all old, for one thing, and awfully realistic-looking. Near me a Rapunzel-haired marionette hung from wires, her long blond braids plaited from human hair, her heavily painted face almost a caricature of a fairy-tale princess. She had a rosy three-cornered smirk that told me she knew what Rapunzel was *truly* like, never mind the story.

"What do you think?" Walker said, handing me my crutch. "I'll bet you've never seen anything like this before, have you?"

"Well, no…what *are* all these things?" I goggled around the room, amazed, awed and more than a little terrified. No wonder Aunt Gray didn't want to come in here. It was like the *Twilight Zone* revisited.

Every available inch of space was crammed. There were jack-in-the-boxes that resembled the jester in the hallway, highly lacquered with cynical grins on their painted faces. Clowns tumbled next to Oriental boy-dolls, while a huge Howdy Doody ventriloquist's dummy perched on a drum. I counted another half-dozen jesters on sticks—one with the face of Queen Elizabeth I, her balding forehead festooned with loops of pearls, a starched ruff surrounding frizzled red hair. Near the diamond-paned double windows, a lit cabinet displayed smaller treasures—tiny tin figures at the wheel of turn-of-the-century cars, iron banks, music boxes in whimsical shapes like carousels and Humpty-Dumpty sitting on his wall. There was more here than I could take in with a single sweeping glance. It was overwhelming.

"These are all toys," Walker explained, making still another transformation to college professor. "A colleague of mine at the university where I work gave me the Maxfield Parrish jester in the hall. I teach folklore, you know, though my speciality is European fairy tales.'' I didn't know, but somehow wasn't surprised. If he had confessed to being a high-wire walker in a carnival, I wouldn't have batted an eyelash. ''The jester grew on me, you could say. That was the beginning of a fascination with old toys. Gray and I rummage through odd little shops whenever we get a chance. That's where I found most of these.''

I realized I was expected to make a comment at this point. ''Everything looks so old. I bet this stuff is worth a fortune.'' Probably one of these dolls, like the Rapunzel marionette, cost as much as the vacation that my mother and I had to give up this summer.

''Yes, some of the dolls are priceless,'' Walker said. ''It depends. For instance—'' He stepped over to a case where some nasty-looking puppets hung from hooks. ''This particular set of Punch and Judy puppets is quite rare. The dolls were used in street theater, which was popular in England during the early nineteenth century.'' He smiled at my blank look. ''Punch and Judy were husband and wife and their plays were rather, well...crude. A lot of smacking with sticks and so forth. The Keystone Cops were tame by comparison.'' I could believe it. Under Punch's big nose twisted the most evil grin I had ever seen.

I was growing more exhausted by the second, but Uncle Walker was just hitting his stride. I propped my crutches against the end of a bookshelf, nearly falling over a carved wooden genie hovering over a tarnished brass Aladdin's lamp. Angel hair swirled from his red-sashed waist down to the spout of the lantern, effectively covering the metal brace that held the doll in midair. He was perfect to the last detail, from his requisite gold earring to the fake-amethyst-studded turban.

''Walker, dear,'' Aunt Gray said hesitantly. ''Couldn't this wait until morning? Holly looks very tired—''

''Young people don't get tired,'' my uncle said firmly. ''Why do you suppose they show old people in those Geritol ads? Now over here you will see mechanical tin toys from Lehmann. Did you know the earliest manufactured toys came from Germany? They weren't for children, you know. The first toys were commissioned by rich people, for their amusement. It wasn't until the 1800s that the average child could play with ready-made toys, if his parents could afford them."

He rattled on another ten minutes about the Charlie McCarthy doll he'd bid on at an auction and lost, then pulled down from a shelf a cardboard box with a picture of a World War I biplane on the cover and the words Lindy Hop-Off emblazoned across the front. I tried to look attentive, but my eyelids were fluttering with fatigue.

"This is a game from Parker Brothers," he said. "Twentieth century. I have some older ones, but these interested me because they reflect the news of the day. When Lindy flew the Atlantic, every kid in America wanted to be a pilot. This one—Siege of Havana—was inspired by the Spanish-American War. Toys mirror our lives and times."

My own life felt as though it were melting into the stone floor. If I didn't get to a bed soon, Uncle Walker could add a life-size Holly Highsmith doll to his collection.

"I'm sure Holly would like to go to her room now," Gray said. She flicked me a sympathetic glance, sidling toward the doorway, as if the dolls gave her the creeps, too.

"Just one more," Walker said, like a little boy begging to watch another cartoon on television. "Look at this, Holly. Do you know what it's for?"

If it didn't have a mattress and blankets, I could care less. He tugged me over to a contraption shaped like an old-fashioned balloon, the kind Jules Verne went around the world in eighty days in. There was a coin slot and what appeared to be a mouthpiece connected to the machine by a long tube.

"Got a penny? Never mind—I have it set so it works without money." My uncle bent over the mouthpiece, drew in a breath that should have sucked half the dolls off the shelves next to the machine, then exhaled with enough force to blow down the three little pigs' houses. In the center of the balloon, behind a glass panel, was a miniature balloon, set against a painted sky full of unlikely constellations. When Uncle Walker let loose his mighty breath, the miniature balloon slowly rose. The stars lit and the man in the moon smiled with glowing teeth.

Despite my near collapse, I had to laugh. "That's great, Uncle Walker! I love it! Can I try?"

His face was redder than the clown's nose. "You'd better wait," he gasped. "Takes lots of practice. It's called—called a lung tester. Used to have them in penny arcades. But they—they were banned after a tuberculosis epidemic. Everybody had to use the same mouthpiece, you see."

"Walker, it's very late," Gray pleaded. "I'm showing Holly her room now. You have to rest yourself."

Too pooped to protest, my uncle wheezed his goodnights.

"I'm sorry about the stairs," Aunt Gray apologized. "All our bedrooms are on the second floor. I hope you can manage." She picked up my suitcase in the hall and led the way up a dark, steep staircase that would have challenged a mountain goat.

"It's okay," I said, maneuvering my cast one step at a time. "I've gotten pretty good at navigating this thing." Just get me to a *bed*, I wanted to scream.

At the top of the stairs I suddenly remembered something. I hadn't seen my cousin. At the airport and on the drive down I only gave a passing thought to the fact that only my aunt and uncle were there to pick me up. I asked Aunt Gray, "I haven't met Alexandra yet. Is she home?"

She had the grace to flush with embarrassment. "She's in her room. She said she'd see you in the morning."

"Is she sick?"

"No. She just—she spends a lot of time by herself. She's a solitary child."

Was that so? Here I'd traveled a thousand miles and she couldn't even be bothered to come out of her room to say hello! The only cousin I had in the whole world! I was beginning to understand the problems Uncle Walker had hinted at in his letter inviting me to stay this summer. No wonder Alexandra didn't have many friends. She probably was terribly stuck-up.

Not only that, but Alexandra had seen me. Someone had turned on the porch light as we pulled up in the driveway. Alexandra had probably spied on us as we got out of the car, decided she didn't like what she saw and gone back to her room. For some reason, that image of my cousin disturbed me.

My aunt stopped at a doorway from which diffused lamplight filtered softly into the passage. "The bath is across the hall—you and Alexandra will share it. You'll find clean towels

on the shelf over the tub. If you need anything else, just let me
know. I hope you'll be comfortable."

"I'll be fine," I said. "I'm so tired I could sleep hanging on
a nail. But I think I'll try the bed tonight." I glanced at my aunt
to see if she got the joke. She wasn't even smiling. Was everyone in this house so glum?

"We're just down the hall," she said, "if you want me."

"The room looks perfect," I reassured her. "I'll probably
sleep like a top." Having said that, I checked out the place the
instant Aunt Gray closed the door behind her. Thank heavens
none of Uncle Walker's funny stuff was in here. No dolls, no
spiteful faces staring at me. In fact, the room looked quite
normal.

I changed my clothes, scuttled into the bathroom for a hasty
face wash, then gratefully fell into bed. I had sat so much that
day, on the plane, in the car on the way from the airport, that
I was stunned my backbone didn't creak like the Tin Man in the
Wizard of Oz.

As I drifted off to sleep, I wondered if all those dolls in Uncle
Walker's toy room were whispering among themselves.

The soft edges of the first light of day slipping into my room
and a distinct feeling of unease woke me early the next morning.

I didn't know what the routine of Blackbird Keep was, but I
had to get out of the house. For all I knew, Uncle Walker spent
the night in a coffin or haunted graveyards until dawn. Turning on the lamp so I could see to dress, I saw my room for the
first time without the hindrance of fatigue-fogged eyes.

It was really very pleasant. All the color in the room seemed
to have been cued from a larkspur-blue matted print hanging
over the antique bed. The same bright blue was repeated in the
handmade quilt and the lemon-yellow and blue calico curtains
at the double windows. A rag rug in the same hues covered the
polished planked floor. The print was reflected in the dressing-
table mirror, which was dim and lavender-tinted with age.

After I made my bed, no small feat on crutches, I leaned over
the headboard to get a better look at the picture, half expecting it to be something gruesome. It was a dreamy watercolor of
an animal unpacking a picnic basket on a riverbank, while an-

other nattily dressed animal lolled under a tree, watching. After a few seconds I recognized Mole and Rat from *Wind in the Willows*, a book I'd positively devoured when I was ten. The blue-checked cloth Mole was setting the food on lent a homey, inviting touch to the scene, making me want to step into the picture, until I realized that the tree Rat lay under was leaning over the picnic and that the artist had painted the bark to form menacing features. The signature scratched in the left-hand corner revealed the artist was Arthur Rackham. Never heard of him.

But the picture proved one thing: nothing about Blackbird Keep was as it appeared. Even a simple picnic had sinister overtones.

No one was up yet. The house was so quiet that my ears roared inside my head as I negotiated my crutches down the steep staircase without making a sound. I didn't like the idea of poking around downstairs in a strange place, but felt nobody would mind if I explored the grounds. I passed the toy room with an involuntary shudder, thankful Uncle Walker kept the door shut and locked. The thought of all those eyes staring sightlessly into the darkness made me hurry out the front door.

Outside, the whole world had submitted to the balmy lushness of June, a startling contrast to the mysterious, Hansel-and-Gretel feeling inside the house. I stood on the wide porch, aware that summer was breathing softly down my neck.

Garden gates brushed against the porch banister, dropping a few of their little purple flowers on the steps like offerings to the goddess of summer. A spider web as big as an archery target was suspended between the porch post and a lilac bush. Jewels of dew glistened along the lacy strands and a fat black-and-yellow-spotted spider worked industriously in the middle of the web, busily wrapping a hapless fly for a midmorning snack. From the treetops, birds chittered and tossed snatches of song into the sweet-scented air.

The sun was coming up over the house, peeking over the sharply pitched roof and pointing up a snarl of twigs and sticks stuffed into the stone chimney that rose from a wing to the right of the main structure. The windows on that side of the house were nearly lost in a thick veiling of English ivy. A wing on the left balanced the symmetry of the house, but the bricks were smoother and brighter, the stones of the corresponding chimney not quite matched, as if the chimney had been attached much later than the other wing.

So this was the house my grandfather had bought for his bride. I wondered what my grandmother had thought of it, isolated on this bramble-embroidered hill, so far from the village. Had she been lonely? If she had, it wasn't for long—not with three rambunctious boys running around. One of those boys had been my father, now dead ten years. One was Uncle Walker, the strange, staid college professor. And one had disappeared, never heard from again. Both my grandparents had passed away. And still the house kept its vigil on the hill, unmarked by time.

I followed a herringbone-patterned brick path that wound around the lilac bush, giving the spider a wide berth. The yard was a real mess. Last year's leaves, sodden with dew, stuck to the bottom of my cast. The grass was whippet thin and so tall it leaned over, as if ashamed to stand up and show how long it had been neglected. Honeysuckle vines strangled dogwood saplings, and an ancient weeping willow that had been given free rein trailed sweeping branches over half the backyard.

There was a little building of some kind behind the willow. I could just see the top of a small peaked roof that had surrendered to the smothering grasp of wisteria. A gazebo? Or maybe a summer house where my grandmother might have served lemonade on lazy July afternoons?

I adjusted my crutches and started down the weed-choked path to investigate, when something black and enormous launched itself at me from the willow tree like a guided missile. I screamed and ducked, nearly breaking my other leg in the process.

Hoarse laughter overhead told me it was safe to look up again, though I couldn't stop shaking.

Caw! Caw! Caw!

It was a crow. An ordinary black crow had dived at me, practically causing me to die of fright. And now it was laughing at me! What kind of a place *was* this, where innocent people were attacked by birds?

"It's all right," a voice said behind me. "Jinx won't hurt you. Although if you want to wring his scrawny neck, it'd be fine with me."

I turned to face a girl my age, with long black hair and the famous Highsmith tea-colored eyes appraising me from beneath dramatic straight black brows.

"You must be Alexandra," I said, still not recovered from my scare with the crow. "Did you call that bird by a name?"

"And you're Holly." Her tone was matter-of-fact, unrelieved by even the faintest hint of warmth. "'Jinx,' yes. He masquerades as a pet, but mostly he's a pest. He's forever picking on Alaric."

"'Alaric'?" All these strange names were swirling through my head. Who was Alaric? A brother they kept shut away in a closet or locked in a tower somewhere? With this family, you could never be certain.

"He's my cat," Alexandra explained. "Jinx pecks at him and chases him all over the place. The poor animal is afraid to leave the house half the time." She raised a small fist to the crow, still cackling at us from his perch. "If you don't cut it out, Jinx, you're going to find yourself in a pie one of these days!"

I took this opportunity to regard my cousin. She was taller than I was and more slender. Her wonderful satiny hair fell sleekly to her waist like an Indian princess'. Her clothes were odd—not campy, funky odd, but just plain ugly, as if she didn't care what she threw on when she got up. She wore a muddy-looking denim skirt, a torn plaid hunting shirt that would have been rejected by Goodwill and red socks bunched over battered Roman sandals. Except for her hair, she looked like a refugee. Delicate, fashionable Aunt Gray had to wince every time she saw her dowdy daughter.

"It seems funny meeting you after all these years," I said, aware I had been staring at her. "I still can't believe I'm not back in Indiana. Mom and I were really surprised to hear from Uncle Walker. We haven't exactly been a close family."

"Daddy believes we should keep to ourselves. It's sort of a tradition. Highsmiths have always been aloof, set apart from the peasants in the village. Blame it all on our grandfather."

I was dying to learn more about Seth Highsmith, but this wasn't the time. I needed to get to know my cousin better, though her sour-pickle expression told me this would not be a small task. "Does everyone call you 'Alexandra'? It's a pretty name, but it's such a mouthful."

"Only Daddy calls me that. To everyone else I'm Zandra."

"'Zandra.'" I tested the two syllables. It sounded so exotic, like something out of the *Arabian Nights*. "Gray, Walker, Zandra, Alaric—" I ticked off the names, wondering if a Mary or John had slipped into the family tree someplace.

"Don't forget Seth," Zandra reminded me. "Our grandfather's real name was Seaforth, did you know that? But he went by Seth."

"Uncle Walker says he called this house Blackbird Keep because he used to study birds."

"That's right," she said, flipping her hair back. "Old Seth was half potted. He didn't just study birds—he trained them. Blackbirds, crows, even blue jays. He kept some of them in that old aviary out there." She indicated the hidden building I had been heading toward when Jinx dive-bombed me. "His favorites were allowed to fly free. He had them so well trained that they stayed around here, usually waiting for a handout. The first bird he tamed was Edgar Allan Poe. That's what's left of his nest in the chimney up there. Granddad would never let anyone clean it out, even though Daddy told him it was a fire hazard. No one uses that fireplace, anyway, because it's in the toy room. So the sacred nest stays."

"What about Jinx? Where did he come from?" I asked, casting a wary eye on the bird, who was cleaning the toes on one outstretched foot.

"Oh, that scamp's been here for years. He's the last bird Granddad trained. He raised the nasty creature from a hatchling. He wouldn't leave even after Granddad died. We'll have to shoot him to get rid of him."

Jinx flew down from the willow tree to land on a cracked birdbath near me. He fanned his tail as he teetered on the edge of the basin, cocking his head to look me over. In the sun, his feathers glinted purple and azure.

"He likes you," Zandra declared. "He sees that you've survived the joke he played on you, so you're okay in his book."

Just what I've always wanted—to rate with a crow!

Then the bird did the most amazing thing. He opened his beak and yelled, "Hold the pic-kle! Hold the let-tuce!" His intonation was a little strange, but the words were perfectly understandable.

I turned to Zandra in amazement. Despite the fact the bird had scared the bejabbers out of me not five minutes ago, I was impressed. "He talks!"

"Unfortunately," she said wryly. "When he's in the house, you can't shut him up."

"What was that he just said?"

"It was an old commercial. When Seth was alive, Jinx used to stay in his room and listen to the radio. Crows are mimics, you know. He can't say anything original, only repeat what he's heard. He knows about a zillion jingles that he picks up from TV and the radio."

A bird that recites jingles! What next? The crow lifted a blue-black wing and stuck his head beneath the feathers, as if overcome by modesty.

"Neat." Words failed me. "A trained bird. I still can't get over it."

"You will the first time Jinx chews up your panty hose."

"Well!" I didn't know what to say. "One thing for sure, this will not be a dull summer. I'm glad I came."

Zandra's brows rushed together. "Are you? Well, I'm not. I know why my father invited you to stay with us and I don't like it one bit!" In a whirl of black hair, she spun around and ran back to the house.

"Zandra!" I called. "Come back! It's not what you think—" She kept right on going, and my explanation died in my throat.

What had gotten into her? I thought she was loosening up a bit, since we seemed to be having a nice, natural conversation. And now this. She probably thought I came because her father sent for me to straighten her out, but it was really more a matter of my needing a place to stay while my mother went to school. Zandra wasn't about to listen to reason, though.

Would I ever be able to figure out these people? Did I want to?

"You deserve a break today!" Jinx croaked.

I had to agree.

Chapter Three

After Zandra ran back to the house, I went inside myself, feeling as unwanted as a piece of gum stuck to somebody's shoe. Aunt Gray called to me from a distant room I assumed to be the kitchen, and I hobbled down the long stone passageway in the direction of her voice.

Now that sunshine slanted through long windows at the front and back of the house, the hall was bright enough for me to see pictures lining the walls like a mini art gallery. There were a half dozen or so on each side, murky watercolors in heavy, ornately carved frames, depicting such scenes as fairies flitting across a firefly-twinkled stream...or dressed field mice unloading baskets of harvest apples while trees, leafy heads bent together, conspired in the background. All the prints were signed "Arthur Rackham," the same signature as on the picture hanging over the bed in my room.

I was particularly taken with one that showed real people for a change. Four children, two girls and two boys, wearing old-fashioned bathing costumes, stood on a crescent of pebbled beach, a strong breeze whipping the girls' hair, the purling sea lapping at the knees of one boy. Although the children looked a little stilted, like a drawing I might have done, the older girl caught my eye.

Her arms were uplifted, as if she were trying to push back the wind that blew her long blond hair or fend off something else... growing up, maybe? Poised on the brink of adulthood, the girl appeared uncertain; innocence seemed to hang in the balance. With their sand shovels and fishing rods, the younger children were safe—they could play at the sea's edge forever. But the older girl looked bewildered and even a little alarmed at the prospect of becoming an adult.

For some reason, I was reminded of my father. What had it been like growing up in this house, especially after his mother died? Did he feel like the girl in the picture—his childhood over too abruptly before a big wind came and blew him into the next stage of life?

Suddenly it was important for me to know him, to learn about Arthur Highsmith as a boy, how he spent his years before he married my mother. Zandra did not want me here and I wasn't wild about the idea of staying here all summer myself, but as long as I was here, I would unearth my father's past. And I would start right now.

The kitchen of Blackbird Keep was a delightful surprise. I had half expected a squat black stove and lots of smoke-grimed brick, like something out of "Snow White." But my aunt was bustling between a stainless steel cooktop and an oak trestle table, cheerily set with red place mats and blue-and-yellow pottery plates and mugs.

"Good morning, Holly," she greeted me. "Zandra said she found you outside. Did you sleep well?"

"'Morning. I slept fine, thank you."

"You didn't get chilly, did you? I forgot to tell you there are extra quilts in the bottom drawer of your dresser."

"I wasn't cold at all. Just right." I tried to make myself look useful, which isn't easy on crutches. "Is there anything I can do? I'm not much good at carrying things, but I can stand at the stove and scramble eggs or something."

Gray threw me a fleeting smile as she set down a platter of sausage, then hustled to the refrigerator. "Don't be silly. You're our guest. Sit down, dear. It'll be a few minutes before we can eat."

The kitchen was actually a great big room that covered the whole back of the house, with the appliances at one end, the trestle table in the middle and a cozy arrangement of couches and chairs at the other end. A television stood on a refinished trunk and the light fixtures were old-timey punched tin lanterns that had been electrified.

I scuttled over to a gingham-covered chair, catching one crutch on the rolled edge of the braided rug. Stumbling, I nearly knocked over an enameled coffeepot holding a bunch of buttercups and black-eyed Susans. "Sorry," I said, righting the pot before I pitched the whole thing to the floor.

"Don't worry about it, dear. I'm sorry our house is so inconvenient. You never realize until someone is disabled—" She broke off to pour milk into a white pitcher.

Remembering my resolve to find out everything I could about my father, I asked Aunt Gray if she knew my father very well.

She shook her head sadly. "Both Arthur and Merton had left by the time Walker brought me here. Seth lived alone, with his birds…and his memories." Without elaborating on that cryptic remark, she went on hurriedly, "I wish I had known your father. Walker always spoke highly of him. They weren't as close as brothers could be—probably because of the age difference. Still, they had each other and they needed that kinship because their father was often difficult, even more so after his wife died. Those boys didn't have much of a childhood, I'm afraid."

I wanted to ask more, but Zandra came in then and plunked herself down at one end of the table. She grabbed a fork and speared a sausage cake.

Her mother, bringing over a pot of coffee from the stove, admonished her. "Zandra, we have a guest. Show Holly where she sits and wait until everybody is at the table before you start eating."

The contrast between mother and daughter was even more pronounced, now that I saw the two together. Zandra still wore the hunting shirt and denim skirt, only the shirt looked even more disheveled, if such a thing was possible. Aunt Gray looked as fresh as an ad for bubble bath in a lilac blouse and a sea-green flowered skirt. A strand of creamy pearls peeked beneath the neat collar of her blouse, just like June Cleaver, the bandbox-perfect mother in the *Leave It To Beaver* reruns, wore while she washed windows.

Zandra glowered at me, as if she resented being reminded of my presence. "You sit there," she said, ungraciously flopping one hand to the oak chair opposite hers. "I'm starving," she told her mother. "Isn't Daddy down yet?"

"He worked late last night," Aunt Gray said. "He wanted to catch up on the time he lost driving to Wilmington to pick up Holly. You know how he is—a stickler for schedules." Aunt Gray's English accent was very faint but still discernible. She said "schedule" without the hard *c*, which made a commonplace word sound charming.

But then the implication sunk in. I stopped unfolding my napkin to look at my aunt. "I hope Uncle Walker didn't have to take time off from work yesterday. I'd feel awful if he did." In my house, only emergencies were considered important enough for my mother to leave work early.

Aunt Gray brushed away my concerns. "Don't fret, Holly. Walker is on sabbatical from the university. He's writing a book—a collection of original fairy tales that the head of his department has been encouraging him to write for years. Now that he's actually got a contract for it, he's anxious to get it finished."

"A collection of fairy tales? You mean, like in Grimm?" I asked.

Zandra swiped another sausage cake from the platter and crammed it into her mouth while her mother's back was turned. "You got it. *Grim* is the word for it."

"Zandra, that is no way to talk about your father's work," Aunt Gray chided.

"You call that work? Making up fairy tales? Why can't he do something really important, like be a lawyer or an architect?"

I stared at my cousin, astounded. Not only was she running down her father at the breakfast table—an act I would have been crucified for if I'd behaved that way in front of my mother—but she was criticizing her father. *Her father.* Where did she get off determining which career was important or not important for him? Granted, writing fairy tales and teaching folklore did sound a bit limp compared to building skyscrap-

ers, but somehow it suited Uncle Walker, and anyway, didn't
Zandra have a roof over her head? Did she spend hours in
conference with her parents, deciding which bills should be paid
and which could wait, or how they should spend their income-
tax refund? I'd bet that ugly hunting shirt she didn't contrib-
ute anything to her family except grousing. Zandra was spoiled.
I had no patience with spoiled kids, though there used to be
days when I wished my mother had pampered me.

Aunt Gray raised an apologetic eyebrow at me. "You'll have
to excuse Alexandra, Holly. Sometimes she forgets her manners." I was willing to wager Alexandra had never learned any.
A regular Emily Post dropout.

Zandra opened her mouth to retort, but whatever she was
going to say was lost in a commotion down the hall. The front
door banged open and shut and Uncle Walker swore grandly in
three languages. A whoosh of wings heralded Jinx's appearance in the kitchen. He rounded past my ear and landed nim-
bly on a T-shaped wooden perch, the kind parrots sit on.
Attached to the perch was a plastic scoop filled with water and
clamshell-shaped cuttlebone. Jinx began innocently gnawing
the bone.

"That blasted bird!" Uncle Walker stamped into the kitchen,
waving a folded newspaper. "He was waiting for me this time.
As soon as I bent over to get the paper, he flew in over my
head."

"This is Jinx," Aunt Gray said formally, as if introducing an
old friend.

"We've met." I eyed the crow cautiously.

"Yeah," Zandra said. "Jinx did his kamikaze number on
her. Scared her half to death. Then he decided he liked her."

"A rare honor, Holly," Aunt Gray allowed. "Jinx barely
tolerates any of us. Consider yourself privileged."

"Is anybody listening to me?" my uncle stormed. "Stop
babbling about that bird as if he's one of the family! Look what
he did to my paper!" He opened the newspaper. The first page
of every section had been methodically shredded, as if the crow
knew that all the good stories began on the front pages.

I coughed back a laugh.

Walker sat down at his place and Aunt Gray hastily poured
his coffee. "Good morning, Holly. I'm sorry you have to wit-

ness Jinx's pranks on your first morning, but it's difficult to prepare people for a nuisance like that crow."

"It's okay. I kind of like him."

"Then you can take him with you when you leave," Zandra said darkly.

Aunt Gray pulled out a chair and began passing a basket of muffins. "For goodness' sake, Zandra. Holly just got here. Don't talk about her leaving already."

Believe me, August couldn't arrive soon enough for me, either. The ten weeks I had to stay here until my mother finished her course stretched before me, endless as the Sahara Desert, a vista made even grittier by Zandra's flagrant dislike for me.

Breakfast was a spectacle. Jinx left his perch the instant Uncle Walker stopped cussing him and proceeded to turn a perfectly normal meal into a three-ring circus. He fell into our teacups, picked at muffin crumbs, pulled Zandra's long hair, snatched at my fork, all the while walking carefully along the edge of the trestle table, just out of cuffing range. I laughed so hard my sides hurt. It was so funny—the bird so obviously had those people over a barrel.

"We've tried to get rid of him," Aunt Gray explained, grabbing her napkin away. Jinx hung on and they tussled until she freed it from his beak. "We even pawned him off on a friend of Walker's who lived miles from here. But he came back."

"Like a curse," Uncle Walker muttered.

"I think he's Grandpa Seth's reincarnation. He hangs around here to make sure we don't sell any of his horrible junky furniture," Zandra put in.

Her father waggled a stern forefinger at her. "You will not refer to your grandfather with disrespect. And the furniture he left us are valuable antiques, not junk. You should consider yourself lucky you get to live in a house like this."

"Yeah, lucky."

Jinx broke the tense moment by leaping on my shoulder. He startled me so I dropped a forkful of eggs.

"He really must like you," Aunt Gray observed. "He hasn't perched on anyone's shoulder since his master passed away."

Once I got used to his sharp claws digging into my flesh, it wasn't so bad. He poked around my ear, nibbling at the gold hoop I wore in my pierced ears. "Ow!" I cried when he tugged at the loop.

Walker leaned across and flicked the bird's tail, so he let go of my earring. "Crows like shiny objects. Gray and Alexandra have learned the hard way not to wear jewelry around the house."

I would remember that in the future, if I planned to keep my earlobes in one piece. Still, I was fascinated by the bird. He was so smart. He figured things out in a matter of seconds. My uncle took a plastic pillbox from his shirt pocket, opened it, took out a yellow tablet, then closed the box and set it on the table while he drank a swallow of juice. Jinx fixed his beady black eyes on the box. Then he waddled over and opened the plastic catch exactly as my uncle had done, flipping the lid back deftly with his beak. He had one of the yellow tablets, when Walker realized what he was doing.

"You don't need a sinus pill," he told the crow, taking the tablet away from him and putting the box back in his pocket. "You really have to be on guard when this fellow's around. He eats anything. Even newspapers."

"Especially the front page," I said, feeling pleasantly full of eggs and sausage.

Jinx had the last word on the subject. "This Bud's for you," he croaked. Breakfast was over.

I hadn't made much headway in my goal to learn about my father. I wanted to talk to my uncle before he disappeared into his study. But Zandra leaped up from the table and ran upstairs, presumably barricading herself in her room, and that left Aunt Gray alone with the cleanup. I felt sorry for her. Her husband loved her I'm sure, but he was lost in never-never land and not much help. Zandra was just plain obnoxious. So I stayed and put away small things I was able to carry, like the jelly and margarine, and kept Aunt Gray company. I think she was grateful.

"You don't have to do anything," she protested at first.

"I want to," I assured her. "I'm not used to sitting around this much. Since I broke my leg, it's driving me crazy I can't help around the house."

"Your mother depends on you quite a bit, doesn't she?"

I picked up the napkins that lay scattered on the table. "I suppose. It's more of a two-way street. I depend on her—she depends on me. Isn't that the way it should be? It's not physically possible for her to work and run the house and do everything else, too. The world doesn't owe anybody a living, she says, so we have to do for ourselves. I'm not wild about that philosophy, but I think she's right."

My aunt took the folded napkins from me and dropped them into a laundry basket in one corner. Her hazel eyes were thoughtful. "And I think your mother is a fortunate woman to have a daughter like you."

Her praise made me uncomfortable, especially since I suspected she was contrasting me to her own daughter. Even though Zandra was a royal pain, it wasn't fair to judge a person by the merits of someone else.

"Is there anything else I can do?" I asked, suddenly anxious to find my uncle.

"No, dear. Run along. You'll undoubtedly find Zandra in her room. She spends most of her waking life in there. I wish . . ." Whatever she wished she didn't confess, but smiled, instead.

"Is it okay if I talk to Uncle Walker? I won't bother him, will I?"

"Oh, no. Walker is used to interruptions. His study is in the wing opposite the toy room. Just knock and go in."

As it turned out, my uncle's study door was open. I tapped on the door frame to get his attention. He looked up from the sheaf of papers in his hand.

"Excuse me, Uncle Walker. Do you have a minute?"

"Of course. Come in, Holly."

I hobbled into the room, careful for once not to trip over the marble threshold.

"Sit down." Walker pointed to the one chair not piled with staggered stacks of papers and books. "Just let me get my house in order first."

While he struggled with his papers, I glanced around. The room was huge, filling the entire wing. Deep-set mullioned windows looked out over the sloping front yard, bringing the lushness of summer indoors. Built-in bookshelves, jammed with more books than I had ever seen in my life, clambered from the floor to the ceiling on the three windowless walls. Beneath the windows was a massive mahogany desk on which sat a battered manual typewriter. Orphaned in one corner was an Apple computer, the monitor screen dusty with disuse.

Between the bookcases were several pictures. I craned my head around to study the one nearest me, which portrayed Mother Goose and her gander riding in, of all things, a rubber tire. Her scarf billowed out behind them and puffy white clouds attested to the fact they were high in the air. What a peculiar picture to have hanging in one's office. But, then, nothing about this house could be measured on a normal scale, including its inhabitants.

"That is an advertisement Maxfield Parrish did for Fisk Tires," Uncle Walker commented, noting my interest. "It was done around 1919. I have another Parrish over here, if you like his work."

He showed me a framed cover for a magazine called *Collier's*, dated 1910. A giant sat on a boulder, holding a young man, probably a prince, in his hand. Just over the giant's shoulder was a castle. These pictures were very different from the Rackham prints in the hall and in my bedroom. Instead of the dreary tones Rackham favored, the Parrish pictures were filled with a light pouring in from an unseen source. I looked at the *Collier's* cover more closely. There was something familiar about the giant's long jaw...

"The jester," I cried. "He reminds me of that jester thing you have in the hall."

"The doll was carved by Parrish," Uncle Walker confirmed, and then I remembered him telling me that last night. "His work is easily recognized because his figures share certain similarities. And his painting techniques, of course."

This was all well and good, but I didn't really want to spend the whole morning discussing the strange pictures in Blackbird Keep. I wanted to find out about my father, but I wasn't sure how to approach my uncle.

"Just spit it out," my mother always urged whenever I had a problem. "Life is too short to waste time beating around the bush."

Following her advice, I stated baldly, "Uncle Walker, can you tell me what happened between my father and my grandfather? I mean, I know a little about their argument, but I don't understand how that would keep them angry at each other for so many years."

"What do you know?" he asked, his smooth forehead crinkled with consternation. I guess this was the last thing he expected me to inquire about.

"Just that my father and Merton were in love with the same girl and that my grandfather thought Daddy gave this girl some heirloom."

"That's all there was to it," he said, discovering a stack of papers on his desk that had to be straightened at that moment. "It was one of those sad circumstances of life when father and son quarrel over some imagined slight. Arthur died before he could make up with Father."

"Are you saying that this missing heirloom business was all in my grandfather's head?"

"Oh, the brooch vanished, all right. It was really a question of who took it. Father had good reason to believe it was Arthur. Since I wasn't there at the time, I only have my father's word to go on."

"But couldn't it have been Merton just as easily? If they both loved the same—"

"Holly, I really must get back to work," he said abruptly.

I knew a dismissal when I heard one. "Certainly." I gathered my crutches and swung around. Getting information from my uncle was not going to be a piece of cake.

Before I reached the door, he called me back.

"I forgot to tell you—Alexandra is driving into the village before lunch. You're welcome to ride along."

"Are you sure it's okay?" I wondered if we were talking about the same girl.

"Listen, I know she's a little prickly, but once you get to know her she's a nice kid. She doesn't seem to have any friends, and I was hoping you could kind of, you know, show her how to get along with kids her age. I want her to be more like—well, more like you."

I would rather kiss a cobra than try to turn the Bride of Frankenstein into Miss Teenage America, despite the endorsements my aunt and uncle were lavishing on me. But an opportunity to get away from this house was too appealing to ignore.

Zandra was waiting in the car by the time I combed my hair and changed into a nicer skirt and top. Now that it was daytime, I could see the car was a hulking black tank of an automobile. Last night I had been too keyed up to notice. It looked like something a British diplomat would drive to Parliament.

"Hurry up, this car is like an oven already," Zandra complained. "And it's not even eleven o'clock."

I fumbled for the door handle, which seemed to be attached upside down, and threw myself into the front seat before Zandra let out the clutch and we took off with a spine-snapping jerk.

"What kind of a car is this, anyway?" I said, running my hand over the cracked leather upholstery. "It's neat."

"It's an English car called a Daimler and it's about a thousand years old. I hate it. I feel like I'm driving a hearse." With her long black hair and melancholy outlook, she belonged behind the wheel of a car like this. "I don't know why Daddy can't drive a regular car, like a Ford. No, we always have to be different."

"What's wrong with that? I'd rather be different than exactly like everybody else." We were going along at a good clip. The breeze through the windows thrashed my hair like a Mixmaster. It did me a lot of good to comb it.

"Easy enough for you to talk. You're like the other guests we've had. They ooh and ah over the quaint furniture and those ghastly pictures, tell us how lucky we are to be surrounded by real Americana, then go home to their normal houses with toilets that work and still lifes on the walls and they probably laugh at fuddy-duddy Professor Highsmith and his oddball family."

That was a pretty harsh view of things. In a way I couldn't blame my cousin—Blackbird Keep *was* awfully gloomy. But she did little to brighten the place, and anyway, she had no cause to run down her parents. Not five minutes ago Uncle Walker was telling me how concerned he was over his daughter, and here she was calling him names.

I couldn't hold it in anymore. "You shouldn't talk about your father that way."

"He's not *your* father."

"You ought to be glad you have a father," I returned, teeth clenched to keep from hitting her.

"I don't know why you came here," Zandra said. "I didn't ask you to come."

"Believe me, if I had any choice in the matter, I wouldn't be here. But since I am, I intend to find out what really happened between my father and Seth." I figured I had nothing to lose by divulging my goal to Zandra.

"Is that so?" she asked. "Well, if I were you I wouldn't snoop too much. You might not like what you find."

"What's that supposed to mean?"

Zandra concentrated on making the turn into Draper's Heights. "Forget it. But if you're looking for clues, you can start in your room. It used to be your father's, I understand."

She didn't say another word until she parked the Daimler in front of the library on Main Street. Switching off the engine, she regarded me levelly.

"Let's be honest with each other. I don't like you and I can see the feeling is mutual. When we're not at home, we don't have to pretend to be the Bobbsey Twins. I'm going to run some errands. I'll be back in two hours. Meet you at the car." Scooping her purse off the seat, she was gone.

I wasted five minutes of my two hours of freedom fuming. Then I got out of the car and scuttled down the sidewalk, heading for the library. The steps loomed above me, seeming to extend for miles.

"Need any help?" offered a voice as warm and rich as hot fudge.

I looked up at a pair of midnight-blue eyes smiling at me from under a fringe of thick sun-streaked bangs. "I'm Kyle Thompkins," the boy said. "You look like you could use a hand." He was the best-looking creature I had seen in ages. Tony Leotta became a distant memory next to this guy.

"Actually, I could use another leg, but a hand will do." The heat must have gotten to me to make a remark that stupid to a boy as drop-dead gorgeous as Kyle Thompkins.

He laughed and the world seemed to tilt at a crazy angle. Suddenly I felt as if I had fallen into a deep hole. I could see a scrap of blue-blue sky and nothing else.

"Are you visiting here?" Kyle asked.

"How did you know?"

"Draper's Heights isn't big enough to hide a new face, especially one as pretty as yours."

I nearly stumbled as he guided me up the wide granite steps. "I'm all right, really. Once I get started I can manage stairs just fine."

"Then humor me. Hey, I told you my name, but you haven't revealed your identity yet. Do you have a name?"

"Holly. Holly Highsmith."

He stopped, the hand gripping my elbow tightening. "Did you say 'Highsmith'?"

"Yes. Do you know my uncle? I'm visiting there for the summer."

"I'm well acquainted with the Highsmith family," he said, his voice suddenly icy. "You're right. You manage the steps quite well." Releasing my arm, he spun on one heel and walked briskly away, leaving me standing on the library steps.

Chapter Four

Have you ever felt on some days that you've gone out the door with a sign pinned to your back that says Kick Me?

That's just the way I felt when Kyle Thompkins left me teetering on the library steps.

It was bad enough that Zandra had abandoned me in a strange town. Okay, so Draper's Heights wasn't exactly a metropolis, but it was still a new place and I didn't know my way around. On top of that, I had a broken leg. Zandra could have put herself out a little by at least pointing out the handicap ramps or something. But because her parents had invited me to help her rejoin the human race, she had it in for me. That I could almost understand.

But this guy Kyle!

He turned against me the instant I told him who I was. My very name caused his jaw to harden and those magnificent deep-blue eyes to darken like a thunderstorm just after dusk.

I know he must have really liked me before he learned my identity, or else he wouldn't have paid so much attention to me. It wasn't just my broken leg…he was definitely interested. He looked just like Tony Leotta did when I told him that one day

I might throw all caution to the wind and start betting at the racetrack—a perked-up expression of surprise, as if he were seeing me for the first time and liked what he saw. Despite the ten pounds of plaster and Mixmaster-whipped hair, I think Kyle liked what he saw, too.

But then I had to go and do something stupid like telling him my name.

Highsmith. What connotations did that slightly snobby surname have in this town that I didn't know about? What other grubby unpleasantries would I encounter before the summer was over? And even more important, would I ever find out what it was about my name that made Kyle Thompkins chill me out?

Mulling over these questions, I crabbed back down the steps, my interest in going to the library—in living, even—dissolved, now that Kyle was gone. Amazing how fast a guy could get under your skin.

It was unbearably hot. An avenue of elms lined Main Street, but the sun was directly overhead and shade was scanty. I wanted to find a drugstore where I could drown my sorrows in a diet soda and browse through fashion magazines. A few people passed me on the street. Usually I ask directions instead of floundering around, but because Kyle and Zandra had made me feel like Typhoid Mary, I decided to find the drugstore on my own.

It wasn't far down the street—a Rexall tucked between a dry cleaner's and Wesley's Bakery. The streaky window displayed faded samples of hair tonics, plastic combs and compacts wrapped in what looked like packages from the fifties. Apparently Draper's Heights was the town that time forgot.

This was even more evident when I entered the drugstore. An overhead fan stirred the air inside. Yet though it must have been close to ninety degrees outside, the air conditioning had not been turned on, if indeed the store had air conditioning. I made my way between narrow aisles cluttered with cough syrups and tins of aspirins, until I reached a marble soda fountain. I debated sitting at the counter, but the high, turntable stools required a dexterity impossible on crutches, so I opted for one of the tiny ice-cream-parlor tables that were grouped at one end of the counter.

Pulling out a wire-backed chair—the wires bent to form a heart shape, naturally—I noticed only one other occupant—a dark-haired young man slowly eating a dish of chocolate ice cream, a folded newspaper propped against the chrome napkin holder. He wasn't as devastatingly handsome as Kyle Thompkins, but he had funny winged eyebrows that gave him a devilish look, like the boy next door who gives you a hotfoot but gets away with it because he's so lovable. This guy had that quality.

He felt my gaze and glanced up at me with a smile.

Embarrassed, I pretended to study the twirly pink-and-gray-flecked Formica tabletop. I wished I had grabbed one of the magazines in the rack on my way back here so I would have something to stare at. Eating out by myself always made me feel self-conscious, as if everybody were watching me, waiting for me to do something dumb like drop a big dollop of mashed potatoes in my lap or slurp my soup.

The counter boy, a pimply-faced kid about my age who immediately made me lose my appetite for pizza for the next nine years, came around with a grease-stained menu. I was disappointed he wasn't wearing one of those soda-jerk hats they wore back in the fifties.

The menu, which was encased in food-spattered plastic and had evidently been typed by someone who'd learned to spell in Liechtenstein, listed the usual BLTs and hot dogs with a side of fries, plus some startling items like Cantelope Sundae and Grape Lemonade. The prices were even more astonishing. Rock-bottom cheap. Suddenly the place became very appealing.

"What'll you have?" the counter boy asked, wiggling his pencil over his order pad as if he needed to psyche himself up before he could write the first letter.

"Ummmm. I'll try the Lime Cooler," I said, all intentions of limiting myself to diet sodas flying out the window. "Is it made with lots of sherbet?"

He nodded and scurried back behind the counter, where he stood a few seconds, undoubtedly trying to remember how to make a Lime Cooler. I prayed he wouldn't mistake a mildewed tennis ball for a scoop of lime sherbet.

"Don't worry," the stranger sitting at the next table reassured me. "Once he gets his brain jump-started, he'll fix a Lime Cooler the likes of which you've never tasted."

"That's what I'm afraid of. What makes you so confident? I notice you're sticking to pretty safe stuff," I replied, grateful someone in this town hadn't taken a vow of silence against me.

"This is true. Some days I don't feel particularly adventurous." He indicated the empty seat next to me. "Do you mind if I join you? I hate to finish chocolate ice cream alone. Also, if I see you coming down with the symptoms of ptomaine I can get you to the hospital faster."

Why not? What harm could there be in having ice cream with an attractive stranger in a place as innocent as Rexall's on Main Street? After all, Lana Turner was discovered by a talent scout while she was sitting in a drugstore in Hollywood. Even if this guy didn't turn out to be a movie scout, he could help me pass the time enjoyably.

By the time he'd moved his newspaper and mostly empty dish over to my table, the counter boy had returned with a pale-green drink frothing over the top of a gallon-sized soda glass.

"Oh, my goodness. I'll never be able to drink all that."

"I'll help you," my new friend said amiably. "Could we have straws, please?"

"I can't share a soda with you. We haven't been properly introduced," I said, lowering my eyelids as demurely as Scarlett O'Hara.

"Victor Denton." He unzipped the paper from his straw. "Now you tell me your name and that should do it."

I experienced a flash of déjà vu—Kyle Thompkins asking me my name on the library steps, then running away from me. "It's—Holly," I said simply.

"Holly what?"

"Just . . . Holly, for now."

"Okay, Just-Holly-for-now. Shall we dive in?" He unwrapped a straw for me and stabbed them both into the drink.

I noticed the newspaper sitting under his ice-cream dish. "Did somebody declare war on us? You were reading that paper as if your life depended on it."

"It does, in a way," Victor replied, dabbing his napkin at the pale-green mustache that garnished his upper lip. "I'm a reporter for the *Sentinel*—that's the paper that covers Draper's Heights and outlying towns.''

"You mean there's enough going on around here to support a newspaper?''

"Absolutely. I'll have you to know I spend every Thursday gathering news for the society section alone.'' His grin told me he was teasing. "It's obvious you aren't a native. I take it you are a visitor to our fair village?''

"Yes . . . and no. I'm from Miller's Forks, Indiana. But this summer I'm staying with my aunt and uncle, who live just outside of town.''

"Really? Who is your uncle? I might know him.''

I didn't want to tell Victor. I had already ruined one potential friendship by revealing I was a Highsmith. Still, he asked a legitimate question—I could hardly put him off.

"His name is Walker . . . Highsmith. He and my aunt live in that big house on the hill a few miles from here.''

Victor frowned. "Highsmith . . . I think I've heard the name, but I don't know him. Sorry. You see, I've only been here about a year. The paper keeps me pretty busy—haven't had a chance to meet all the locals.''

"Oh,'' I said, relieved the Highsmith name hadn't poisoned Victor as it had Kyle. "Well, if you'd like I could introduce you to my uncle sometime.''

"I'd like that,'' Victor said blandly. I sensed he was merely being polite. What could he and Uncle Walker possibly have in common?

Suddenly I remembered Alexandra's two-hour edict. "Do you have the time?''

Victor checked his wristwatch. "Five after twelve. Are you getting hungry for lunch?''

"No. I mean, I have to get back. My cousin said she'd be ready to leave about this time.''

"For a minute there I thought you might turn into a pumpkin. I'll walk you to the car. Make sure you don't fall in any potholes along the way.'' Over my protests, Victor paid my check, saying that he had drunk most of the Lime Cooler, anyway, and gallantly assisted me down Main Street to the library.

It was wonderful having an attentive guy touching the small of my back very lightly, almost possessively. I half hoped Kyle would be waiting in front of the library, carrying one red rose as an apology, and that he'd see other guys appreciated me, no matter what my last name was. Then I wished the car were in front of the library.

The spot where Zandra had parked the Daimler was empty. She had gone.

"She left me! How could she?" I railed. "She couldn't have waited another five minutes! How am I supposed to get back home?"

"Some cousin you got," Victor declared. "Calm down. My car is right over there. I'll drive you home. Didn't I tell you I run a taxi service on the side? Special rates for pretty girls with broken legs."

Victor Denton was a lifesaver. Not only did he drive me back to Blackbird Keep, but he kept me laughing the whole way. By the time we rolled up in the driveway I didn't care that Zandra had bugged out on me.

Victor whistled when he first saw the house. It had that effect on people. "Some digs. What did you say your uncle does for a living?"

"I didn't. He's a professor. Right now he's on leave from the university because he's writing a book."

Victor acted as if he hadn't heard. He kept staring at the house in rapt fascination.

"Listen," I said. "I'll have to pay you back for coming to my rescue. How about coming by some afternoon for lemonade? You can meet my uncle and his wife. And even my rotten cousin, if I don't murder her first."

"Yes," Victor said slowly, as if waking from a dream. "Yes, I'd like that very much."

Zandra had an airtight alibi. She arrived about fifteen minutes after Victor dropped me off, unconcerned that she had left her crippled cousin in the lurch.

"I only went up the street to get gas," she explained glibly. "When I went back you still weren't there, so I figured you went home with Kyle. I saw you talking to him."

"You know Kyle Thompkins?" I forgot for the moment that Zandra's excuse was as thin as cellophane.

"Of course. He goes to my school. He's a year older than me, so he's in the class ahead."

"Does he—"

"Does he what?"

"Nothing." I wanted to ask her if Kyle acted funny toward her because she was a Highsmith, but then it occurred to me that maybe Kyle disliked Highsmiths because of *Zandra.* If she had hurt him once, that would be reason enough to hate her relatives, especially female cousins with the same tea-colored eyes. Which would make me guilty by association.

Yet there had to be more motivation behind Kyle's behavior than bitterness toward an old flame. He seemed too decent, too sincere, to let pettiness override good manners. Whatever reason the Highsmith name was mud to him, I had a feeling I would find out before the summer was over.

The weather had turned abysmally hot, with no rain in sight. I was so sick of my crutches I wanted to throw them down the hill, and my cast, always a burden, suddenly became a torture. My leg itched fiendishly. I stuck pencils and letter openers between my cast and skin, trying to scratch, but to no avail. Being covered with honey and staked to an ant hill was nothing compared to this misery.

Life at Blackbird Keep fell into a routine. Aunt Gray slipped unobtrusively around the house, cleaning and cooking. My uncle worked in his study all morning and afternoon.

Zandra bolted herself in her room, playing records from the sixties on her stereo. Once she left her door open, and when I passed by, I saw a copy of *The House of Mirth* lying facedown on her unmade bed. I also had a glimpse of piles of clothes everyplace, scarred maple furniture and one wall painted black. A black cat, undoubtably the crow-harassed Alaric, regarded me with unfriendly yellow eyes. He looked like a feline version of Zandra. No wonder she read depressing stuff like Edith Wharton. I was beginning to see more each day why Zandra had no friends.

When I wasn't devising new ways to scratch my leg, I sat on the front porch, listening to the drone of bees in the peonies and longing for home. My ten-week exile yawned before me, a chasm wider than the Nile. Mom sent me a postcard from Olive Branch. The photograph showed a steamboat paddling down the Mississippi. Mom scribbled that this idyllic picture was a myth, at least at the training institute, which sounded like a cross between Sing Sing and the lost city of Atlantis. She had no time for magnolias or mint juleps, her instructors kept her so busy.

I didn't see much of Jinx for a few days. One afternoon when I was hobbling around the backyard, contemplating taking a hacksaw to my cast, the bird pulled his dive-bomb number. He still scared me, but at least this time I knew what it was. Again he laughed at me from the willow tree, enormously pleased with himself.

"Very funny," I said sourly. "I bet if somebody did a survey, they'd find the life spans of people living around here are shorter than anywhere else in the country."

He flew over to perch on my shoulder. I had sensibly stopped wearing earrings. He made funny little cooing sounds in my ear. Rascal that he was, I couldn't help liking him.

He rode on my shoulder while I uncovered a rust-bitten wrought-iron bench near a sagging toolshed and sat down. While I absently picked clover flowers and tossed them in a little heap at my feet, I wondered why my uncle didn't take better care of the place. He seemed proud of the house and furnishings, yet the grounds were like an Amazonian jungle. Surely he earned enough as a college professor to hire a boy if he didn't want to do the work himself. Or maybe having an unkempt yard deterred unwanted visitors. Since I had arrived, no one had come by to chat or even deliver a package.

Jinx hopped down and began picking clover flowers, too, waddling over with them in his beak to add them to the pile. I noticed the bird was careful to sort out the fuzzy pink blooms from other wildflowers. He copied my movements exactly. It was a little unnerving.

"Do you like me?" I asked the bird. No one else seemed to in this house. Aunt Gray was lovely but distant. Uncle Walker made the right gestures, but they were hollow. And Zandra probably had a Holly Highsmith voodoo doll hidden in her room. After almost a week here, I felt like the man without a country.

"Are you my friend?" I enunciated every consonant, trying to get the crow to repeat what I said. "Are—you—my—friend?"

He cocked his head and stared at me. "Where's the beef?" he replied.

"Where, indeed?" I sighed.

Popular or not, I still had a mission to fulfill. Blackbird Keep held the clues to my father's past. Solutions to family secrets were wrapped in these walls, waiting for me to unravel them.

I went back indoors, determined to find out something.

On this particular afternoon the house was quiet; only the muffled, rhythmic tap-tapping of Uncle Walker's typewriter sounded from behind the closed study door.

I looked for Aunt Gray in the kitchen, but she wasn't there. A pot of spaghetti sauce simmered on the stove. She couldn't be far—the sauce would have to be watched. My aunt had a little sitting room beyond the stairs where she wrote letters and did needlepoint. Perhaps she was in there.

As I passed the toy room, I noticed the door open a crack. This was unusual, because my uncle diligently kept it locked. I supposed Aunt Gray went in once in a while to dust.

Gingerly I pushed the door open and peered inside. The ivy-cloaked windows blocked the afternoon sun. The dolls sat motionless in the gloom.

"Aunt Gray?" I called tentatively. No reply. Pushing the door open all the way, I could see she was not there. Neither was Uncle Walker. It wasn't like him to leave the room unlocked. Maybe he needed something from his collection for his book and wanted to get back to work quickly before inspiration dried up.

All those dolls spooked me, sitting so calmly on their shelves, staring, staring at nothing. Or at me. I had no business going into an off-limits room—apart from the fact that toys gave me the willies—but the same power that brought me to Blackbird Keep in the first place now compelled me to break the house-guest's unwritten code of ethics and snoop around.

What was it about this room? It wasn't just the toys, though heaven knows a thousand painted faces would be strange enough in anybody's book. Some force drew me in here with the same sense of urgency I felt in Uncle Walker's letter. It wasn't my uncle's stiffly worded invitation, but another, more commanding voice, as if someone had used Walker's letter as an instrument to speak through. Someone who couldn't contact me himself because he was too far away. . . .

Suddenly I knew.

Seth.

I was feeling my grandfather's influence in this room. And the vibes were definitely hostile.

As I turned to go, I experienced another sensation—eyes boring into my back. An absurd notion, I know, considering the number of dolls, but these eyes felt *real*. A gargoyle mask leered down at me from above the door. I broke the ten-yard-dash-on-crutches getting out of there.

Aunt Gray's sitting room was a welcome sanctuary. It looked just like her—soft and undemanding, a quiet retreat. No toys or Rackham pictures in here. A chaise upholstered in celadon green lounged on plush silver carpeting. Flowers in driftwood shades papered the walls, giving the room a dreamlike, underwater atmosphere. Soothing touches of celery, silver and charcoal were found in vases, figurines and paintings.

My aunt was seated at a dainty rolltop desk, writing a letter on heavy pewter-colored stationery. She had a lonely, tragic air about her, like a queen in a fairy tale waiting for the king to come home from the wars. All she needed was a wolfhound at her feet.

I drew a deep breath and cleared my throat, announcing my presence. Aunt Gray looked up, startled.

"Holly, I didn't see you there. Come in, please."

"I don't want to bother you—"

"Oh, pooh. I'm tired of writing, anyway. It's practically a full-time job, answering letters from my long-winded friends in England."

I sat down on a damask-covered wing chair. "Do you miss England much?"

Her lips curved into a gentle smile. "Not really. I've been away so many years—this is home now." A little frown marred her porcelain forehead. "Is something wrong? You looked a little strange when you first came in."

Much as I wanted to confide in her, I couldn't let anyone know I had been fooling around in Uncle Walker's toy room. "It's just that—" I stopped, encouraged by her concern, and began again. "Aunt Gray, I wish I could find out about my father...why he left and why he never came back."

She sighed. "Oh, dear. I'm afraid you're asking the wrong person. I'm still a newcomer to this family."

"I've tried talking to Uncle Walker, but he—well, he puts me off."

"I think that's because he feels guilty. You know all the trouble between Seth and your father happened while my husband was still in school in England. When he came back, Seth treated him like the favored son—a role I don't believe Walker ever felt he deserved. I know Walker wishes he had tried getting Arthur and Seth back together. Then your father died and it was too late."

"What about Merton?" I prodded. "Didn't Uncle Walker want Merton back in the family, too?"

Aunt Gray's hazel eyes became colorless, blank, like a dipper of pond water strained of sediments. "Merton was something else again. I know very little about that situation."

I sensed she was about to end the discussion so I quickly asked, "What about the heirloom my father supposedly gave to the girl he and Merton fought over? Uncle Walker mentioned a brooch—"

"That's right. It belonged to Isabelle."

"'Isabelle'?"

"Your grandmother," Gray supplied. "Seth's wife. Remember, she died when the boys were fairly young. Anyway, Seth sent this brooch to his wife when he was overseas."

I recalled Mom saying something about the fortune my grandfather garnered in Europe between the wars. "Was this pin terribly valuable?"

Aunt Gray shook her head. "No. I believe it had more sentimental value than anything. When it disappeared, Seth was furious, as though its loss were an affront to the memory of his wife. That's really all there was to it."

Somehow I doubted that. The disappearance of his wife's treasured pin was probably a sharp blow to my grandfather, but hardly a sufficient wedge to drive father and son apart for the rest of their lives.

After supper I went upstairs to my room to wash out a few pieces of lingerie. A breeze kicked at the curtains and I went over by the window to drink in the first cool air in several days.

Zandra had told me this had once been my father's room. Funny, but I couldn't detect his presence the way I received my grandfather's vibrations in the toy room. Had so much time passed that his impression had eventually dissipated, like the memory of a rare and wonderful perfume? Or was my grandfather's personality more dominant? Too bad—I would have liked to commune with my father's spirit.

The windows overlooked the backyard. From here I could see the shabby garden, the monstrous willow and Zandra's cat as he cakewalked around the birdbath in that prissy way cats have. Jinx swooped down out of nowhere and buzzed the cat. His wings grazed Alaric, who flattened his ears and belly-crawled across the yard like a well-practiced guerilla fighter.

I was about to turn away, when a flutter of white near the abandoned aviary captured my attention.

A strange woman wearing a gauzy white gown drifted down the overgrown path, hesitating between a rambling rosebush and the aviary as if she didn't know which way to go, like a restless phantom unable to return to her grave.

Chapter Five

For an instant I thought the woman was Aunt Gray. But I had just left my aunt in her sitting room before coming upstairs to my room. Even at this distance I could see the woman was too small to be my aunt, more frail-looking where Aunt Gray was slender.

Her behavior was definitely weird. She appeared to be looking for something, a lost object dropped among the high weeds, perhaps. Her robe flapped in the breeze like a white flag of truce. Perhaps this woman was a neighbor, though I hadn't observed any houses closer to Blackbird Keep than two or three modest homes on the state road we took into Draper's Heights.

In case Uncle Walker had a real thing about people trespassing, I decided either he or Aunt Gray should know about this woman doddering around their backyard.

Zandra came out of her room the same moment I did. We nearly collided in the narrow hallway. She looked annoyed, as she always did whenever she saw me.

"You never told me who drove you home," she said, as if our conversation earlier had taken place only seconds ago.

"You never asked," I flung back.

"That's because you were more interested in Kyle Thompkins." Zandra had an unerring talent for needling people in their most vulnerable spots. I felt the jab where it hurt most, just as she intended. "But I gather he wasn't the one who brought you back here."

"You gather correctly. The guy's name was Victor Denton. You know him?"

Zandra shook her head. "Never heard of him. Is he new in town?"

"Sort of. He said he'd been here about a year. He's older, so you wouldn't know him from school. He works on the paper. He's really nice."

My cousin lifted a ruler-straight eyebrow. "You met two boys in less than two hours in a perfectly strange town?"

I couldn't resist rattling her cage. "And with a broken leg, too. You should see how fast I move with *two* good legs." Then I remembered the woman in the garden. "Listen, there's a lady out near the aviary. I saw her from my window. Is she somebody who lives near here?"

"What are you talking about? Nobody lives on this hill but us." She made it sound like the sort of information documented in a renowned travel guide.

"How should I know who your neighbors are?" I said peevishly. Zandra managed to distort the simplest exchange of dialogue until it became an argument.

"We don't have any. The closest people are the Hansens, and they live in that yellow house before the turnoff."

"That's more than a mile from here. Is Mrs. Hansen an older woman, by any chance?"

Again Zandra shook her head. "They're a young couple. Their kids aren't even in elementary school yet."

A peculiar feeling, like the way leaves sense an impending storm and turn up their pale-yellow undersides, coursed through me. "Come look out my window," I told her. "There's a woman prowling through the garden."

For once Zandra didn't squawk in protest, as she followed me back into the guest room. The blue-and-yellow calico curtains stood out like banners as a stiff breeze poured through the screens, brisk and refreshing as a bucket of mountain spring-water.

"She's right next to—" I broke off, stunned.

There was no one by the old aviary. The yard looked as deserted as always. Hazy twilight misted the riotously overgrown rosebushes that spilled over the splintered, paint-chipped trellises like mischievous boys escaping out a schoolroom window. The garden seemed undisturbed, as if it were paralyzed under a hundred-year enchantment and still had fifty years to go.

"I don't see anybody," Zandra said, leaning on the sill to gaze out over the yard.

"Well, she was there a few minutes ago. I saw her!"

"Really? Then where is she? There's no place to hide, unless you count that old pot lying on its side. She'd have to be pretty small to crawl in there," she remarked, her disbelief laced with sarcasm.

Her abrasiveness made me jangly. Leave it to Zandra not to take me seriously. "Of course she's not under that pot," I snapped. "I tell you, I saw a woman down there. She was wearing something white and floaty, like a robe."

"What, no bell, book and candle? A woman in white, right out of a Wilkie Collin's novel. Are you sure you don't have a touch of heatstroke, Holly? I hear it makes people imagine things."

"I didn't imagine it! I saw her! Why would I make up something like that?"

Zandra shrugged with studied nonchalance. "Who knows? If you see the Headless Horseman, please don't bother me. One ghostly vision a day is enough."

We glared at each other, light-brown eyes clashing with light-brown eyes, the same and yet so different. At that moment I didn't want to claim Zandra as my cousin. "You can't choose your relatives," Mom told me once. From the way Zandra bored holes into me, she wouldn't have picked me, either.

She left, her unspoken views hanging in the air like stale cigarette smoke after a party. She thought I was crazy, and I suspected she was lying. Although she covered it well, I believed Ms. Alexandra Highsmith knew a lot more than she let on. The woman in white, whoever she was, was no stranger to Blackbird Keep. I'd bet my next broken leg on it.

The following afternoon Victor Denton came to call. Aunt Gray was amazed when he knocked on the door, bearing a box of Whitman's chocolates and a manner bordering on Edwardian courtliness, but no one was more dumbfounded than I.

"Holly asked me over," Victor explained glibly through the screen door. "To meet you and Mr. Highsmith and perhaps have a glass of lemonade."

I remembered exactly what I'd said. I had asked Victor to drop in *sometime*, not practically five minutes later. And certainly not before calling first to see if it was okay to come over.

Brushing her hair back in a flustered gesture, Aunt Gray gave me an I'll-talk-to-you-about-this-later glance, then invited Victor inside.

"Please come in, ah—Mr.—"

"Denton. But call me 'Victor,' please. Hello, Holly," he said when he saw me standing next to the brass elephant-leg umbrella stand. "Is that your new cast?"

I smiled weakly at his joke. "Not hardly. Victor—how nice to see you again. I'd like you to meet my Aunt Gray—I mean, Mrs. Highsmith." I performed the introduction clumsily, but Victor's sudden appearance on our doorstep had startled me. "Aunt Gray, you remember I told you about the nice young man who brought me home the other day when Zandra left me—"

Victor broke in smoothly, "Holly and her cousin got their wires crossed. A little mix-up about times. Holly seemed concerned, so I drove her home."

"That was very kind, Mr. Denton," Aunt Gray allowed.

"'Victor'—please." He presented her the box of chocolates with sweeping gallantry. Sir Walter Raleigh could have taken lessons from him. "When Holly mentioned you make the best lemonade in Delaware, I bought these. Chocolate and lemonade compliment each other, don't you agree?"

"Not half as much as you do," I wanted to say. Talk about laying it on thick. I refrained myself from asking him where he kept his trowel. What was he up to?

Aunt Gray accepted the candy graciously, then excused herself to go into the kitchen and whip up some of her famous lemonade. This last said with a meaningful look at me: "Holly, why don't you take Victor out on the porch? I'll call Zandra down." To Victor she said, "I'm sorry my husband can't join us. He's working in his study and he left strict orders not to be interrupted today."

Victor's smile faded with disappointment. "That's too bad. I really wanted to meet Holly's uncle."

"Some other time." I didn't mean that to sound rude, but I was still taken aback by Victor's tactics, barging in unannounced like an insurance salesman. "The porch is this way," I told him, all but shoving him out the door.

I needn't have worried. Victor was the perfect guest. He was witty, informed, and so captivating that even prickly Zandra succumbed to his charms. Aunt Gray made a huge pitcher of lemonade that truly was wonderful, and the four of us demolished both layers of the Whitman's Sampler, laughing and talking like old friends. Victor's job at the newspaper had provided him a crash course in the area, and his anecdotes about learning the ropes in Draper's Heights were liberally sprinkled with nuggets of gossip, which Aunt Gray adored.

At first Zandra stumped downstairs in one of her usual sulks. But all Victor had to do was flash a deep-dimpled smile at her and she was conquered. I think she would have thrown herself under the wheels of a passing train if he'd asked her to.

"Mrs. Highsmith, where have you been hiding these gorgeous girls?" Victor gushed. "Of course Zandra takes after her lovely mother. But I've never seen cousins with the same bewitching eyes before."

"It's a Highsmith family trait," Aunt Gray said, glowing with maternal pride. He had her then—hook, line and sinker. As much as I liked Victor, I wondered if he had been a snake-oil peddler in another life.

"I am fascinated by this house," Victor admitted after a while. "Could I see it? If it's not too much trouble."

Sufficiently jollied by flattery and chocolates, Aunt Gray waved a hand as if she were bestowing a blessing. "Certainly. Zandra, will you give our guest a guided tour? Just steer clear of your father's study."

"I'll go, too," I said, struggling with my crutches. It wasn't that I was jealous of Victor's attentions to my cousin. Not at all. Well, maybe a little. After all, hadn't he first been bewitched by *my* tea-colored eyes in the drugstore?

Zandra threw me a look fierce enough to shrivel plutonium as Victor helped me up. His protective touch on my elbow made me feel special again.

I introduced Victor to the jester in the hallway and somehow wasn't surprised when he seemed familiar with the work of Maxfield Parrish. Entranced by the Rackham prints and the Chippendale furniture, both of which he correctly identified with no more than a cursory glance, Victor was naturally intrigued by the toy-shop sign.

"It's locked," I told him, not wanting to go in there ever again if I could help it. "My uncle keeps it locked. We're not permitted in there unless he's with us."

"Don't be silly," Zandra said. "I can go in anytime I want."

While Victor was engrossed in the Rackham seashore picture, I watched Zandra tip the umbrella stand and feel underneath the elephant's foot. A glint of brass disappeared in her hand.

So Zandra had access to the toy room. Could she have left the door open yesterday afternoon? If she had, why hadn't she locked it when she left? And what was she doing in there?

Victor's face registered astonishment, amazement and unabashed delight, in that order, when Zandra ushered him into the room. "This is great!" he cried. "Now I'm dying to meet your father," he told Zandra. "Any man who collects such wonderful old things is someone I want to know!"

Zandra pointed out the more unusual items, such as the Punch-and-Judy set and the Queen Elizabeth jester, but her knowledge wasn't much more extensive than mine. Victor found the balloon lung tester and couldn't resist blowing into the mouthpiece. When the stars and man in the moon lit up, he turned to me with triumph shining in his eyes. It was then that I noticed Victor's eyes weren't cocker-spaniel brown as I'd originally thought, but a deep, unfathomable black, like a bottomless pool of India ink.

After that first successful visit Victor became a regular caller at Blackbird Keep. The next time he came, two days later, he met Uncle Walker, and the two hit it off upon discovering a mutual devotion to the Orioles. Victor never dropped by without a bouquet of carnations or a cheesecake from Wesley's Bakery or a book from the library that Aunt Gray mentioned she'd like to read. And he never let us know in advance when he was coming. "My schedule is pretty hectic," he confessed once.

I sat on the glider with my aunt during these visits, contributing little to the animated discussion but trying to figure out how Victor Denton managed to become so intimate so fast with my aunt and uncle, when even their only niece was unable to work that magic.

"That boy could charm the birds right out of the trees," Aunt Gray remarked after one of Victor's visits.

Not quite. Jinx didn't like him. He reverted to uncharacteristic crowlike behavior when Victor was around, never venturing any closer to the porch than the lilac hedge. He didn't talk, either, but sat in the topmost branch of the bush and cawed sharp warning signals, as if Victor carried a rifle.

Jinx's racket made it somewhat difficult to talk at times. "That darn bird," Zandra would grumble. "He acts like there's a hunter around, the way he's carrying on."

I couldn't help wondering if Jinx's intuitions were right.

The first heat wave of the summer passed after a drenching thunderstorm brought blissful relief. Victor Denton didn't call once that week. By Friday, Zandra's moping threatened to become epidemic, and even Aunt Gray seemed more subdued than usual. I had to admit I missed him, too. No matter how much attention he paid to the others, he always had a special smile just for me. Before leaving, he would squeeze my arm or brush a lock of hair off my cheek, letting me know that I was still number one.

Friday was also grocery day. An excursion to the local Safeway was scarcely high adventure, but after sitting around the house for five days in a row, I desperately needed a change of scenery.

"Zandra drives me," Aunt Gray explained, adding last-minute items to her list, "now that she has her license. I never had any desire to get behind the wheel of an automobile. Is there anything special you would like, Holly?"

"Just to go along. I'm not much use pushing a cart, but I'd like to sit on a bench outside or something."

Zandra immediately suspected me of having ulterior motives. "I suppose you'll just happen to stroll past the *Sentinel* office while we're in the store."

I patted my cast, now dirty and grungy after so many weeks. "Do I look like I'm going to stroll anywhere?"

Her answering smile was as chilly and treacherous as the iceberg that put itself in the path of the *Titanic*. "You manage to get around pretty well."

In the backseat of the Daimler, I mulled over Zandra's sniping remarks. She zinged them at me every chance she got. Even in Aunt Gray's or Uncle Walker's presence. She was so good at it, so subtle, they never caught on. One of these days, I resolved, I was going to march in her room and tell her exactly what I thought of her.

Apparently my aunt and uncle felt I was civilizing their daughter, as I had been enlisted to do. If Zandra dressed less like a bag lady and remembered to say thank-you occasionally, it had nothing to do with me. Victor Denton deserved all the credit. Instead of throwing on an old bathrobe with one sleeve ripped and fisherman's sandals, more often Zandra would appear wearing jeans that weren't too far gone and a blouse that was actually pressed. When Victor pulled up in the driveway, she would bound upstairs to her room, coming back down with her glossy raven hair tied back with a ribbon.

As they used to say in Victorian days, she was smitten with him.

I wasn't sure how I felt about Victor. He was good-looking, unpredictable and a little mysterious—a lethal combination to vulnerable girls like Zandra . . . and me.

Maybe my cousin knew me better than I thought. Did I tag along today just to get out of the house, or was I hoping to bump into Victor? There had been so many strange things to deal with since my arrival—the shock of Blackbird Keep, the toy collection, Jinx, Zandra's hostility, the woman in the garden—that I felt uneasy trusting my own instincts. My world had been turned upside down to the point where days unfolded like scenes in a play... and the script was only revealed a page at a time.

The Safeway was located on the far side of town, several blocks away from the drugstore and the library. While Zandra backed the Daimler dangerously close to a van, complaining that the spaces weren't designed for anything bigger than Matchbox cars, I spotted a park across the street.

"I'll wait over there," I told my aunt. "Now that it isn't so broiling hot, it'll be nice sitting in the sun. Catch a few rays."

The park was really a pie-shaped plot where three streets met to form a triangle. There were two or three shade trees with benches beneath them and a brick walk skirting the edge of the park, rimmed by well-tended petunias and marigolds. The walk also led to a multitiered drinking fountain supported by an ancient cannon thrust upright through the basins of trickling water.

Naturally the sight of sun-dappled water made me thirsty. I hobbled over to the fountain, cupped my hands beneath a glittering spray and drank greedily. A shadow fell over the rainbow-spangled basin. I took one last slurp, which dribbled down the front of my T-shirt and splattered my feet, then hitched up my crutches.

"Sorry," I said to the person behind me. "I didn't drink it all. It only looks that way."

"It looks like you spilled a lot. Maybe you should have tried the dog's fountain."

I knew at once who belonged to that slow, sun-warmed honey voice before I turned around to face him—Kyle Thompkins.

I have always wanted a Grand Moment. The kind where I would say or do something that was so final, so devastating, that it would take the other person years to recover. Unfortunately my Grand Moments are always spoiled, like the time I had a fight with Tony Leotta in the Main Squeeze, a glorified juice bar in Halloway Mall, and stomped out the door with my head high, only to come skulking back five minutes later after I realized I had left my purse hanging on the back of my chair.

Now if this were an old MGM production, I would have curled my lip like Bette Davis, pushed Kyle into the fountain and stalked away, swinging my hips as if I hadn't a care in the world. Being on crutches, however, immediately eliminated two of the three key elements in that scenario. Curling my lip alone would have accomplished little, except making me look as if I had swallowed a fly in that last gulp of water.

I doubt if even Bette Davis would have had the nerve to walk away from a boy like Kyle. With his straight, sun-lightened hair cut in thick bangs, he looked like a California surfer transplanted to Delaware. His jeans were unfashionably faded and the tropical shirt he wore would have been more at home in Malibu than this undistinguished little town.

Totally without finesse, I bluntly asked him, "Are you going to insult me every time you see me? What have I ever done to you?"

The arrow hit the bull's-eye dead center. He actually reddened. "I apologize for that crack about the dog's fountain."

"But not for leaving me standing on the library steps the other day?"

He refused to address that situation. "See this plaque?" He pointed to a small bronze plate attached to the center basin, abruptly changing the subject. "It says this fountain was erected by the Daughters of the American Revolution in 1912."

"Fascinating." I made my tone as sarcastic as Zandra's.

"No, it really is. The cannon came from Chadds Ford, near Brandywine Creek. That's where Washington and Lafayette fought General Howe in 1777, trying to keep him from taking Philadelphia."

My American history was rusty at best, but I didn't feel I had to impress Kyle Thompkins. "And did they?"

He shook his head. "They were defeated at Brandywine, but they won the war, you know."

"Yeah, I saw it on the six o'clock news," I remarked sourly.

"This fountain was designed in three tiers, with the cannon as its main support. Birds were supposed to drink from the top, people and horses from the middle, and dogs used the bottom." He tapped the low shallow basin with one sneakered foot. Now I fully understood his insult.

"Very funny." I adjusted my crutches to hobble away with as much dignity as I could muster. Tears sprang to my eyes. He had really hurt my feelings.

A hand gently took my upper arm. "Hey," he said softly. "I said I was sorry." He searched my face with eyes like the North Sea at night.

I know I presented a scintillating sight—the front of my shirt soaked with water, grubby cast and tears trickling down my cheeks. I didn't even have a Kleenex. Why does disaster always strike whenever a handsome guy is around?

Kyle offered me a bandanna tugged from his back pocket. "It's clean," he assured me.

I mopped my face, then blew my nose with an unladylike snort. "I have to know. Please tell me why you ran away the other day when I told you who I was."

"Let's go sit down." He steered me to a bench under the generous awning of an oak tree. "I shouldn't have reacted the way I did that day at the library. I'm one of those people who act first and think later."

"My name turned you off, didn't it?" I pressed. "Why? Does my uncle have enemies I don't know about?"

"Only one. Me. Other than that, he's a pillar of the community, which is no slouch considering the way his father worked his whole life alienating everyone in town."

"My grandfather?"

"The very same. Seth Highsmith." The twig he'd been fiddling with suddenly snapped in his fingers. "The man who ruined my aunt's life right up until the day he died."

"Your aunt?" Now I was thoroughly confused. "I know my grandfather didn't get along with at least two of his sons, including my father, but I never knew anything about your aunt. Who is she?"

"Her name is Kathryn. And there isn't any reason you should have heard of her. The Highsmiths look after their own, but the rest of the world can go to blazes." He stared at me. "Your father wasn't Arthur Highsmith, was he?"

"Yes, he was. He died when I was six. What about him?"

"He jilted my aunt, that's what. Left her with a broken heart. If that wasn't enough, your grandfather accused her of keeping some pin your father gave her."

Realization dawned. "Not—your aunt—is she the girl my father and his brother fought over a long time ago?"

Kyle nodded.

"The girl from the village . . ." I murmured. It had never occurred to me that this girl would be my mother's age by now. For some reason I pictured her as a young girl still, like a fairy princess who never aged.

"She practically raised me," Kyle went on. "When my parents split up, Mom had to go to work. Aunt Kathryn kept me every day after school until I was eleven—old enough to stay home by myself. She never married, you know, after your father broke up with her. She really never got over him."

"What about Merton?" I asked. "The way I heard it, both my father and Merton liked your aunt."

"I think she was fond of Merton, but nothing like what she felt about your father. 'Artie,' she called him."

"She still talks about him?"

Kyle's tone became sodden with resentment, like a doughnut dunked too long in a cup of strong coffee. "All the time. See, you have to understand my aunt lives in the past. She always has. Probably always will. She's real—emotional. And when Seth started hounding her to give back that pin, she got even worse."

"I don't believe my father ever gave the brooch to your aunt," I stated.

"Yippee," he said flatly. "You're only about five years too late. Seth is dead, but my aunt still feels guilty."

"Listen," I told him, "arguing about this won't do any good. I know so little about my father's family it isn't funny. I didn't even want to come here this summer, but now that I'm here, I intend to find out some things. If my dad and your Aunt Kathryn are innocent, it's up to us to clear their names, right?"

"You and I will find out what really happened twenty-five years ago?" he asked skeptically.

"You have any better candidates?" I had nothing to lose. Kyle could help or he could walk. Either way, it wouldn't stop me from learning the truth.

Maybe he read that in my face. His midnight-dark eyes were guarded, but the look he gave me confirmed a reluctant partnership.

Chapter Six

"There you are, Holly. I've been looking for you." Uncle Walker came into the kitchen.

"I'm having an early lunch," I told him.

I was leaning against the tile-topped counter, eating the second half of a bologna sandwich and feeding snippets of meat to Jinx. The crow stood on the long-necked chrome faucet, which made a good if unorthodox perch, and took the bologna bits from my hand as delicately as if he were having tea with Margaret Thatcher. At first I was afraid of his beak, which was sharp and strong, but the bird didn't behave aggressively around me the way he did the others. He followed me everywhere, indoors and out, even though Uncle Walker tried vainly to enforce no-crow-in-the-house, a law that Jinx repealed at least three times a day.

Uncle Walker frowned when he saw the bird. "What's that creature doing in the sink, for heaven's sake? Shoo, you horrible bird! Go back to the woods where you belong."

Surreptitiously I slipped the last piece of bologna to Jinx. "I'm sorry, Uncle Walker. He rode in on my shoulder. It's my fault. Don't yell at him. And I think it hurts his feelings if you tell him to act like a regular bird. He isn't, you know.''

Two weeks of living at Blackbird Keep had me talking up for a common crow! Another two weeks and I'd probably be defending ants and bugs, advocating insect rights.

"You wanted me?" I reminded him.

"Yes. I'd like to talk to you about Alexandra."

Here it comes, I thought. He's heard us bickering and wants to know why we can't get along. "What about her?"

"Well, first off, I would like to say that she's finally starting to come out of her shell, thanks to you."

"I haven't done anything, really."

"Yes, you have," he said. "Mealtimes are actually pleasant. And we all enjoy sitting on the porch after supper, something we never did before you came. Most of all, Alexandra doesn't spend half as much time closeted in her room, listening to that awful wailing—"

I had to smile. Zandra's tastes, reflected in the dreary books she read and the clothes she wore, were eclectic, to say the least. Instead of rock or punk rock or new wave or even early Beatles, she owned every single Bob Dylan album and played them one after the other, hours on end. I liked the sixties' folk-rock sound as much as the next person, but a little of Dylan's back-of-the-throat twang and heavy-handed lyrics went a long way.

My uncle went on. "She seems to enjoy the company of Victor Denton. Too much. He's a nice enough young man, but I'd rather Alexandra saw kids closer to her own age. She's getting starry-eyed over him, I'm afraid. Doesn't she know any girls? Perhaps you could suggest inviting a few over some weekend for an overnighter or whatever you call them."

"'Slumber parties,'" I supplied, trying to imagine a bunch of giggly girls eating potato chips and playing the Lindy Hop-Off game in the toy room. "Honestly, Uncle Walker, I don't think Zandra is friendly with any girls at school. I've asked her who she hangs around with, but she just shrugs and says nobody likes her."

"And why is that?" He wasn't being smart—he really wanted to know.

How could I tell him that Zandra said she had always been ostracized at school because her father drove a weird English car and taught fairy tales, and her house was funny-looking with all that dark old furniture and a big black crow that at-tacked anyone who came to the door, practically. Zandra hated her life here—that's why she escaped into Edith Wharton nov-els and the adenoidal ramblings of Bob Dylan.

Uncle Walker was waiting for an answer, his wide brow crinkled above his horn-rimmed glasses.

"It's—I don't know," I stammered. "I think part of the problem might be because—because she lives outside of town. Kids hang out after school when they live near one another. She just feels—left out."

"She has her driver's license. She can go into the village anytime she wants, within reason."

"But she's gotten along without close friends all these years," I said. "She's been labeled a loner. It's hard to break that mold. Even if she went into town every day and spent the whole day there, it'd be hard for people to see her any other way." I was oversimplifying, but I didn't feel like going into how kids tend to run in packs and that Zandra would prob-ably have to dynamite her way into a clique.

He looked at me as if I were a new species. "How did you get to be so smart in just fifteen years?"

"Sixteen years. Nearly." I wet a finger to pick up bread crumbs on the counter. Jinx imitated me by pecking at stray crumbs around the sink. "Mom says I was never a kid. After Dad died, I became like a mother to her—it was really strange."

Uncle Walker nodded absently. "I can understand that. I know your mother must have loved Arthur very much. A lot of people miss him . . . sad, he was so young."

The type of cancer my dad had set no age limits on its vic-tims. I tried not to dwell on that. "Life is for the living," Mom would say whenever we both got a bad case of the weepies.

I was touched by my uncle's concern for his daughter. Yet despite his worries, he seldom talked to Zandra, only skim-ming the surface of safe topics. Without heart-to-heart talks with my mother, I didn't know how I could cope. My mother was my best friend in the world. Zandra's parents, for all their love, kept her at arm's length. Maybe the problem with Zan-dra stemmed from a lack of confidence on their part because she was born so late in life to them. Maybe they just weren't used to teenage girls.

A car horn beeped outside. With a jolt I remembered that Kyle Thompkins was picking me up and taking me to meet his Aunt Kathryn. The invitation could in no way be construed as a date—we were partners trying to track down the truth and that was it, which Kyle made crystal clear to me in the park. Still, I had dressed in a pastel-striped cotton jumper with a full skirt that hid most of my yucky cast and had clipped my hair back with peppermint-pink barrettes.

"I've got to run," I said. "I have—I'm going into town for a little while to see a friend."

"Oh, really?" Uncle Walker was surprised that I had made friends in a matter of days, while his daughter remained so unpopular.

I knew he was going to ask who this friend was and I didn't want him to know about Kyle's aunt. Not yet.

"O-R-E-O!" Jinx suddenly shrieked, saving the day. I loved that silly bird. Silently I promised him a handful of his favorite cookies when I got back.

Kyle was waiting in an orange-and-bronze Jeep with the top removed. He jumped out when he saw me hobbling down the steps and opened the passenger door.

The seat was too high for me to manage on crutches. Kyle simply threw my crutches in the back and lifted me up, settling me into the bucket seat. He swung into his own seat, released the brake, and we were off.

It was a glorious day. The sun felt wonderful on my face. Conversation was impossible as we breezed down the state road and I tried not to think about how bald I'd be by the time we reached Kyle's aunt's place. The wind whisked my hair over and around my barrettes, the ends stinging my eyes like lye water. Next time I would put my hair up in a ponytail, if there *was* a next time.

Once inside town limits, Kyle slowed down. Since we could talk without screaming, I attempted to draw him out.

"Do you go camping?" I questioned. I had read in one of my fashion magazines that the best way to get a boy to warm up to you was to show an interest in his hobbies.

"What?"

"The Jeep. I wondered if you used it to go camping."

"Yeah. How'd you know?"

I finger-combed what was left of my hair. "You seem like the type. Where do you go?"

"Cape Henlopen sometimes. Bombay Hook Island. Once in a while Broadkill Beach."

"I've never heard of those places. Are they near here?"

Kyle shook his head as he stopped at the one flashing red light in the center of Draper's Heights. "No. Cape Henlopen is clear down to Lewes Beach. They're all along the coast, but they aren't what you'd call popular resorts. Mostly wildlife refuges. I take off on Friday night, come back Sunday."

"Who do you go with? Your friends? Anybody special?" That was a not-so-subtle way of finding out if he had a steady girl.

"Nobody. The whole purpose in going is to commune with nature. I don't need a bunch of people yakking around me."

A boy who looks as though he stepped from a Coppertone ad spends his weekends by himself in a wildlife refuge? A lone wolf, just like my cousin. I began to wonder if the education system in Draper's Heights stressed individuality to the degree where the town was cranking out social dropouts right and left.

The fashion-magazine advice wasn't working. I abandoned the old share-his-interests strategy and decided to be myself—just plain nosy. "Tell me more about yourself. You said your parents were divorced when you were very young? That must have been rough. I know you're really close to your aunt. Do you have any brothers or sisters?"

"Nope. Just me and my mom. And Aunt Kathryn. She's my mother's older sister."

"What about your father? Do you see him often?"

His laugh was harsh. "My father split when I was a baby. Nobody's heard of him since."

Another missing person! First my uncle Merton, now Kyle's father. Besides the tragedy of his aunt and my father, we seemed to be linked by several common bonds. Still, it was too early in our relationship to jump to conclusions. I glossed over his father's disappearance, sensing it was too painful for idle conversation, and latched onto the fact that Kyle was an only child.

"No kidding. I'm an only, too. I read someplace that only children are supposed to be more self-reliant. It's just as well, since it's been 'me and my mother against the world,' as we say in our house."

"What about your uncle?" He signaled left, then turned the car onto Elm Street, a pretty avenue decorated with freshly painted, enormous Victorian houses that were probably owned by the village's doctors, lawyers and prosperous merchants seventy years ago. Draper's Heights was a real Norman Rockwell town, with its Main Street and Elm Street and turn-of-the-century houses proudly sporting flags in anticipation of Independence Day, just a few weeks away.

"Uncle Walker didn't step into the picture until last month. He came to Daddy's funeral, but then we didn't hear scat from him. To show you how little I know about the Highsmiths, when Mom told me about the fight my father had with my grandfather, that was the first I'd ever heard of Merton. Can you imagine, having relatives you never knew about?"

"No, I can't. But, then, my family isn't as prominent as yours is around here. Have you been able to find out any more since you came?" Now Kyle turned the car onto a maple-shaded lane where the houses were smaller, like honeymoon cottages.

"Hardly anything," I said. "You'd think they'd want to talk about the family, especially since Uncle Walker acts as though the Highsmiths are directly descended from Napoleon. But he's as slippery as a mink whenever I bring up the subject. And Aunt Gray ought to work for the IRS—she's even more evasive than he is. I'm hoping to find out something from your aunt."

Before we left the park the other day I'd suggested meeting his Aunt Kathryn. Kyle wasn't taken with the idea, but I'd convinced him that talking to her was the logical place to start.

My palms were already sweaty. In just minutes I would confront my father's past and meet the woman he loved but left behind.

Kyle stopped the car in front of the last cottage on the street. The house sat well back from the road, surrounded by ancient maples that hovered ominously over the cottage rooftop, like the tree that menaced Mole's picnic in the Rackham print over my bed. Constructed of dingy gray-white clapboard, with tired-looking green shutters, the house seemed to turn a dejected shoulder to its spiffier, well-scrubbed neighbors.

A crippled picket fence meandered around the cramped lot. Dispirited primroses tumbled over a quartz-ringed flower bed, pushed out by bristling chickory and other bullying weeds. The house wore a faded, discouraged air, like a wedding cake that had never been taken off the bakery shelf. This was a cottage in a forgotten fairy tale, tarnished by time and unfulfilled promises. I dreaded going through the crooked gate.

"This—is this your aunt's house?" I asked, hoping Kyle had taken the wrong street.

"Yeah. Pretty bad, isn't it?" He sighed. "I've offered to fix it up for her, but she only let me patch the roof once when a storm ripped off some shingles. I mow the grass and rake the leaves in the fall, but that's about it."

"You mean, she likes it this way?"

Kyle turned toward me, his eyes dark as sapphires dropped down a well. "Holly, before we go in—let me tell you about my aunt. Don't expect—well, she's a little strange."

"How strange?" I swallowed. My mouth was suddenly very dry. "She can't be any stranger than Uncle Walker. Does she have ghastly-looking dolls in her front hall?"

He ignored my attempt at humor. "Remember how I told you she was very emotional? Well, it's like she's on some kind of a roller coaster most of the time. I never know if she's high or low when I visit. She's not crazy or anything . . . just—different. You don't have to be afraid."

"Who's said anything about being afraid? She does know you're bringing me over here?"

"Oh, yes. And when I told her you were Arthur Highsmith's daughter she got very excited. But that was yesterday. Today could be another story."

Having prepared me for the worst, Kyle came around and helped me out of the Jeep. The gate squeaked like nails being yanked from a coffin when he opened it. I noted his frown—Kyle was obviously the type who needed to fix things, whether it was a creaky gate or the broken dreams of a sad old woman. I liked guys who cared. By the time we reached the front door,

I realized I was more intrigued by Kyle Thompkins than any boy I had ever known.

Before he raised a hand to knock, the door was flung open by a smiling woman wearing a fifties-style circle skirt and a yellow blouse. A coquettish ribbon caught shoulder-length blond hair heavily frosted with silver. Her indigo eyes, so like Kyle's, radiated genuine gladness to see us.

"Kyle! And Holly!" she cried as if we were dear friends just returned from a trip around the world. "Come in!"

We stepped through the door into a dim room.

"Aunt Kathryn," he began. "This is Hol—"

But Kathryn clutched both of my hands in hers and exclaimed, "I know who she is! Artie's girl. My dear child, I'd know you anywhere—you look just like Artie."

"Hello, Miss—" With a jolt, I realized I didn't know her last name. I couldn't very well call her Aunt Kathryn.

But she gave a trilling little laugh. "Oh, let's don't bother with formalities. Please call me 'Kate.' That's what your father called me, you know. 'Kiss me, Kate,' Artie would say. Everyone else must call me by my given name, but you can call me Kate."

"Thank you," I had the presence to say, giving Kyle a glance. I wondered why he warned me about his aunt—so far I found her delightful.

"Sit down, both of you," Kathryn chattered. "I've just made a pitcher of iced tea. I'm sure you must be thirsty after that hot, windy drive in Kyle's Jeep. I'll be right back."

"You should be comfortable here," Kyle said, indicating a plump chair with a sagging ottoman. He helped me prop my leg on the stool, then sat down across from me on a love seat protected by an old-fashioned fringed slipcover.

When my eyes adjusted to the gloom of shades drawn in the middle of the day, I saw the room was quite shabby. The carpet was a blue-and-green nubby pile, worn to mesh in some spots and paper-thin where the rubber backing had flaked off, leaving little putty-colored trails of powder that seeped out at the corners.

The chair I was sitting in was once a peppy magenta, judging from the remnants of color still trapped in the seams, but was now a lifeless salmon, the arms stained and darned. On the scratched coffee table was a book of Shakespeare's sonnets, lovingly thumbed until the cover curled softly at the edges.

There were a few knickknacks scattered about. A plastic doll wearing a feathered headdress and nothing else made goo-goo eyes at us from atop a large, boxy television set. A lopsided vase painted a knuckle-clenching chartreuse held a place of honor on a small table under the window. There was a silver-framed picture sitting next to it, but I couldn't make out the indistinct black-and-white figures.

"I don't know what you were so worried about," I whispered to Kyle. "Your aunt is very sweet."

"For now," he returned doubtfully. "It might not last. Sometimes she—"

At that moment, Aunt Kathryn bustled into the living room, carrying a tray on which sat a pitcher of lime-spiked iced tea, three glasses and a plate of chunky oatmeal cookies. "Here we are," she said brightly. "Holly, Kyle told me about your accident. I hope your leg is mending fine."

I accepted the glass of tea she handed me. "It hurt at first, but now the only thing that bothers me is the itching inside the cast. That and those crutches."

"When does the cast come off?" Kyle inquired, biting into a cookie.

"Next month," I replied. "I'll still be here, but Aunt Gray has already arranged for a doctor to see me when it's time." To Kathryn, I said, "These cookies are terrific. They're so chewy I could eat a dozen."

Her bell-like laugh reflected her pleasure. "I knew you'd like them. They're Artie's favorite."

It was unnerving having my father mentioned every other sentence as if he were still alive. While Aunt Kathryn poured herself a glass of tea, I observed her carefully, wondering what my father had seen in this woman twenty-five years ago. She wasn't the young village girl I had originally pictured as a teenage version of Heidi. And she wasn't the haggard, pitiful old woman in the image I'd contrived after seeing the sad little house. Kathryn was probably a few years older than my mother, but by no means elderly.

Her clothes and outdated hairstyle made her seem youthful at first glance, but the impression was fleeting. Even as she lifted the glass to drink, I was aware that her hands, despite girlish pink-tipped fingernails, were wrinkled and lined. She reminded me of a beautiful young girl who woke up one day to find that time had played a cruel trick on her. Unable to accept fate, she still faithfully wore her high-school clothes and long hair in hopes of fooling the calendar.

Suddenly I felt sorry for Kathryn, who wanted so much to be pretty young Kate again. I wished I had never come.

"How's the tea?" Kathryn asked.

"Very refreshing," Kyle replied, setting his glass on the coffee table. He looked at me, and I knew it was time to reveal the purpose of our visit.

I shook my head imperceptibly, trying to signal to him that I had changed my mind. Aunt Kathryn was clearly enjoying the fuss of fixing us tea, as if we dropped in every week for a neighborly chat. To bring up the past now would burst her little soap bubble, and I didn't want to hurt her feelings.

"Will you be in town long?" Kathryn inquired, passing the cookie plate again.

Kyle replied for me. "Aunt Kathryn, I told you Holly was staying here for the summer."

Perturbed, his aunt set the plate back on the tray before either of us could take seconds. "Oh, that's right. Where is my mind today?"

Don't do it, I willed Kyle. Let it go.

But he pushed on. "Holly's staying with her Uncle Walker at Blackbird Keep. It's the first time she's been here."

Like a hairline crack marring a Wedgwood china cup, Aunt Kathryn's smile slipped, blurring her features. "Blackbird Keep?" she whispered.

"That's right," I told her gently. "Where my father grew up. As a matter of fact, I'm staying in his old bedroom."

"He was a wonderful boy." Kathryn's voice was faraway and hollow sounding, as if she were speaking from the vast corridors of distant memory. "Both of them were. I couldn't make up my mind between them." She giggled like a debutante. "Merton was better-looking, but Arthur was the sweetest. I went with Merton first, but then Arthur asked me out. Mert was so jealous he couldn't see straight."

She was silent a moment, her forehead puckered in recollection.

"Aunt Kathryn—" Kyle began, but she stood up and went over to the television set.

"Mert gave me this," she said, picking up the cheap plastic doll. She ruffled the dyed turkey-feather headdress. "Isn't it ugly? It's so ugly it's cute. Mert won it for me at a carnival. He pitched so many baseballs he said he felt as if he were in spring training. But his aim wasn't very good and it took him forever to win anything. Spent a fortune on me that night, he did."

"Aunt Kathryn," Kyle said firmly. "Holly is here because she wants to know about her father. He died when she was very young, you know."

I found my tongue at last. "Yes, if it's not too much trouble for you to remember, I would like to know what happened between my father and my grandfather. Seth."

"Seth!" Kathryn hissed the name the way one would say "scorpion." "We won't talk about Seth. We'll talk about cheerful things, shall we?" She flounced over to the small table where the green vase and picture frame stood. "Artie made me this vase in sixth grade. We went to school together, you know. He had a crush on me even then. Look, here we are at the Fireman's Ice-Cream Social." She brought the silver frame over to my chair to show me, but wouldn't let the picture out of her hand.

The picture was an enlarged snapshot, grainy and amateurish. My father, who appeared to be no more than seventeen or so, sat at a picnic table littered with empty ice-cream dishes. Kathryn, wearing a slim skirt and a blouse printed with poodles, snuggled next to him, practically in his lap. Both grinned like idiots into the camera, obviously deliriously happy.

I didn't like seeing this side of my father—the young, devil-may-care boy who would later become riddled with disease. I brushed the picture away, deciding that I wasn't ready to learn the truth about him. What I wanted more than anything was to go home—my home, not back to Blackbird Keep.

Kyle sensed I was upset. "Well, listen, Aunt Kathryn, it's really been great, but I think Holly is tired. We'll have to be going."

Kathryn set the picture on the coffee table and turned back to me, her face like a shattered mirror. "He loved me! I know he did! No matter who he married, he never got over me! You have to know that!"

No, I didn't. But I couldn't gather my crutches fast enough to make a hasty, if rude exit. I was afraid Kathryn would start crying or screaming or tearing her hair out, and I couldn't deal with it. Now I knew what Kyle meant when he cautioned me against her erratic mood swings.

"He gave me this book!" Kathryn stabbed the book of sonnets with one forefinger. "Doesn't that prove he loved me? He even marked one of the poems. Wait, I'll read it to you—"

I couldn't stand another second of this. Kyle half assisted, half dragged me to the door as his aunt began reciting.

"'Shall I compare thee to a summer's day? Thou art more lovely and more—'"

"What about the brooch?" I blurted. "Kate, tell me about the brooch. Did Arthur give it to you?"

She stopped, her face ashen. "The brooch?" Her voice was thin and brittle, like isinglass. "What brooch?" She drooped, looking like the Rapunzel marionette hanging from wires in Uncle Walker's toy room.

"The one Seth says you kept. Did you?" I asked wildly, with Kyle pulling me toward the door. "Do you have the brooch?"

"No!" She spit out the word. "I don't have it. I never did. Only for a few minutes."

"When?" I quizzed. "When did you have it?"

"Artie brought it out to me one afternoon. It was so pretty— like nothing I'd ever seen before. He pinned it to my blouse. But he said it belonged to his mother and he couldn't give it to me, not just yet. 'I'll wait,' I told him. We were sitting by the aviary. I'll never forget. He unfastened the brooch but then he dropped it in the grass. It took us quite a while before we found it. 'One day,' he said, 'it'll be yours.' I told him I'd wait forever. Forever." Her voice died away.

I realized with a shock that the woman I had seen haunting the garden near the aviary was Kyle's aunt. Had she been trying to relive that wonderful afternoon when my father had promised her that the brooch—and all it implied—would be hers one day?

Was she still looking for the brooch? Or for her lost love?

Chapter Seven

I could tell by the way Kyle was driving that he was angry. I didn't blame him. I was mad, too. At myself. I had gone to his aunt's looking for answers and had come away feeling as if I had brutalized a sick woman, for that's what Kathryn was. No question about it. She was heartsick, to the degree where my father's rejection—real or imagined, I wasn't sure which at this point—had poisoned her entire life, the way one rotten apple spoils the whole barrel.

Aunt Kathryn was haunted, if you can use that word to describe a person. She was plagued by the ghosts of her past and persecuted by a wrathful old man whose accusations reached out beyond the grave. And then I came along—Seth Highsmith personified—and let her have it again. What on earth had made me do it? Was I truly like the grandfather I had never known and never had any desire to meet the more I learned about him?

The silence grew until we were out of town, on the twisting little road that led to Blackbird Keep. Kyle sped up and the wind whipped my hair again, but I didn't care.

He spoke first, banging his fist against the steering wheel in a mixture of guilt and frustration. "I shouldn't have taken you there. I should have realized what was going to happen. Aunt Kathryn just couldn't handle seeing Arthur's daughter. I guess it was like flaunting the fact that he left her and married someone else."

"Please," I said, my eyes closed. "Don't rub it in. I can't describe how terrible I feel. As though I'd torn the head off some little kid's favorite doll. Kyle, I yelled at her about that stupid brooch! I don't know why I did it, except I couldn't stand to hear her talk about Artie another second. Do you understand?"

"I understand you're as bad as old Seth. You took up where he left off." His jaw was grimly set as he concentrated on the road.

That hurt. It was one thing for me to think I might be like my grandfather. It was quite another for Kyle to say so.

"We shouldn't have gone," he said again. "It was a crummy idea."

"You didn't think so the other day. It's not *all* my fault, Kyle."

"I know. We both want to clear this thing up. We just went about it the wrong way."

I summoned the nerve to rest my fingertips on Kyle's arm. "I'm sorry about Kathryn. Will she be all right?" I couldn't tell him I had seen her in the garden at Blackbird Keep. He was upset enough.

He nodded. "She's had these—spells before. I'll drop in on her before I go to work this evening."

"I didn't know you worked. Where?"

"Place called Ed's Garage, down on Chestnut. It's been there a thousand years—used to be a wagon shop that converted to fix horseless carriages. That's how old it is."

"Do you like working on cars?"

"I don't plan on making a career of it, if that's what you're implying. The money's good and the hours aren't too bad. If I want to go to college after high school, I have to put myself through. Nobody's giving me a free ride in this world."

"Me, too. I mean, I'll have to put myself through school, too."

He gave me a quick glance. "No kidding? I thought the Highsmiths were rolling in dough."

"Not the Indiana branch. In fact, that's the real reason I'm staying here this summer. My mother is taking a special class so she can get a promotion, and this was the only place I had to go to. We need every cent we can get."

At the foot of the driveway, Kyle pulled the Jeep over by the mailbox and stopped. "Is there any point in going on with this lunacy, Holly?"

The wind had rumpled his thick bangs into charming disorder. I longed for him to take me into his arms and tell me everything was all right. But that was like asking for pennies to rain from heaven.

"If you put your prejudices against my family aside for five minutes, I think we can help your aunt—and clear up the mystery about my father. But it'll never work if you keep sniping at me. I'll see if I can find some old papers or pictures or something. Start pumping Uncle Walker, if I can."

Kyle sighed. "All right. If there's anything I can do, let me know." But he couldn't resist a parting shot. "One thing for sure, you're undeniably a Highsmith."

By the time I reached my room, I'd begun to resent any attachment to the name. Where was the family I'd so longed for when I was little? All of them—Uncle Walker, Aunt Gray, and especially my cousin Zandra—were a disappointment.

What did Kyle mean when he said I was undeniably a Highsmith? That I was eccentric like my uncle? Or as despicable as my grandfather had been? I couldn't believe that. I was not a terrible person. Sometimes I did things I wasn't proud of, but never intentionally.

When Aunt Gray called me to the telephone that evening, I was lying on my bed, staring at the same ceiling my father must have stared at years ago.

"It's your mother," she said excitedly, as if Mom were calling from Singapore.

The phone was in the recreation area of the kitchen. Aunt Gray and Uncle Walker tactfully left the room so I could have privacy.

"Hi, Mom." I hoped she was calling to tell me the course was over early and I could go home. "What's up?"

"Nothing really. I just wanted to hear your voice. Did you get my postcard?"

"Yeah. You're really whooping it up on the Ole Miss. Is school over?" Even if it wasn't, maybe I could convince her to let me join her in Mississippi or quit in the middle and take me home.

"Not yet. I still have six weeks to go. You're not homesick, are you, Holly?"

"No. Well, just a little." What a lie! If my homesickness were bottled and given to kids as a daily tonic, the runaway rate would plummet to zero.

"Poor baby. Walker and Gray are treating you okay, aren't they? She sounds awfully nice. I talked to her a second."

"She is. So's Uncle Walker. Everything's . . . great."

"Well, that's good." She went on about her classes and instructors and the other students with such enthusiasm I didn't dare mention I couldn't take another night in this house. Mom rattled on a few more minutes, then said she had to hang up and go study.

"Be a good soldier," she said. "August will be here before you know it."

Whatever happened, Private Highsmith was stuck here another six weeks. I had better make the most of it.

The next day I approached Aunt Gray. Since my uncle had taken off after breakfast to spend a day working in his university's library, she was my alternate source of information.

"You came to this house a long time ago," I said after she invited me into her sitting room. "Do you remember if my father left anything? Like old letters or pictures? Or even his old toys?" I had been thinking the night before how nice it would be to have a memento of my father's childhood.

Aunt Gray put down the butterfly-enameled vase she was dusting, flannel rag in one hand. "Toys?"

"You know. Things that might be stored in the attic." I crossed my fingers behind my back, praying this ploy would work. The attic, I was convinced, was the place to start searching for answers, since the occupants were so reluctant to reveal family secrets.

"There isn't anything worthwhile in that attic," Aunt Gray said, sending my hopes in a downward spiral. "Seth cleaned it out a few years after his wife died. Threw away all of his sons' things—toys, school papers Isabelle saved, everything."

"Why did he do that?" Was my grandfather going to foil me at every turn?

She shrugged. "Who knows? Perhaps he didn't want to be reminded of her death, so he went on a housecleaning spree and threw away the boys' things along with Isabelle's possessions. By the time I came here with Walker, the attic was as bare as Mother Hubbard's proverbial cupboard. There isn't anything up there except wall-to-wall dust and cobwebs."

"Surely there are pictures. Seth wouldn't have destroyed pictures of his wife, would he? And what about his papers? He lived a long time after my grandmother died. Aren't those things stored someplace?"

Aunt Gray smiled. "You are definitely your grandfather's grandchild. Persistent to the end."

If one more person told me I was just like Seth Highsmith, I would scream. Instead I mumbled, "I'm sorry. I don't mean to cause trouble."

She tossed down her dust rag and came over to squeeze my shoulder. "You're not one bit of trouble, Holly. In fact, this house is considerably brighter since you came. I only meant you seem determined to learn about your family. That's rare in a young person these days. People ought to care more about their roots." Her soft hazel eyes were like the new leaves of spring misted by a gentle April shower. "I'm sorry you lost your father at such an early age. Despite the loss, you and your mother meet life head-on. I think you're both remarkable people. And I know Arthur would have been immensely proud of you. Seth, too, though he'd rather die than admit it."

I gave her a quick hug. "You know something? You're my absolute favorite aunt in the world." Of course, she was my *only* aunt in the world, but why bring that up? She was such a sweet person under that shield of diffidence. I'd supposed that a lot of her reserve was natural—an Englishwoman still trying to get accustomed to American ways. And yet a good share of her aloofness might have come from that house. There was a somberness within those walls that would have even turned Pollyanna into a wet blanket.

Her ivory-pale cheeks flushed prettily with embarrassment, Aunt Gray said, "There are some papers and even a family album, plus records from your grandfather's bird studies. Walker moved them into his office when he set up his toy collection in Seth's old den."

"The toy room used to be my grandfather's den?"

She nodded with the smallest of grimaces, a slight wrinkling of her nose that signaled how much she disliked her husband's unorthodox collection. No wonder the vibes were so strong in that room. And no wonder I hated to go in there. It's almost as if the dolls and puppets had absorbed my grandfather's hateful personality. I shuddered at the notion that he had the power to change inanimate toys into instruments of evil.

The bright morning sun hadn't reached the deep mullioned windows of Walker's office yet, but fresh air brought in the heady, fresh fragrance of early summer. I smelled a hint of honeysuckle and even the last perfume of the lilacs, which were languishing more each day.

Aunt Gray pulled several folders and leather-covered volumes from one of the shelves. "Feel free to browse through these in here, if you want. Walker won't be back until after dinner. Or you can sit outside on the porch. It's such a gorgeous morning."

I thanked her and sat down in the empty chair, the books and folders piled in my lap, to determine what I had. There was a thick, calf-bound volume that seemed to be an accounting of my grandfather's work with blackbirds, written in familiar-looking scratchy writing. Then I realized Uncle Walker's handwriting style was very similar. I skimmed the stiff, parchment-thick pages, catching the names of birds as I went: Edgar Allan Poe, Nostradamus, Merlin. Seth apparently had a sense of humor, at least employed in naming his precious blackbirds. I put this book on the table next to me, anxious to find something more personal.

There was a photograph album, the pictures carefully anchored on black pages with little triangular paper hinges. Beneath the snapshots were captions penned in white ink. I wanted to study the pictures in a good light, so I set the album aside to take out onto the porch.

The last book appeared to be household records. The first entry was dated August 10, 1928, the year my grandfather went to Europe, according to what Uncle Walker had told me. My grandparents had bought the house earlier that same year. They must have moved in before Seth went abroad, and Isabelle probably kept the record book initially. The neat, swoopy script was the same as the white-inked captions in the photo album. I flipped through the blue-lined pages until I saw the spiky, firm hand of my grandfather, indicating he had taken over the accounts after he returned permanently from Europe.

Aunt Gray had given me three folders—cardboard envelopes the color of dried blood and tied with frayed tapes. Unfastening the bulkiest, I found business letters typed on onionskin paper. Since they seemed to be of the dear-sir-we-are-in-receipt variety, I stuffed them back into the folder and went on to the next.

This one contained letters, too, but they were written by hand, some in Isabelle's writing, others in Seth's—love letters between my grandparents, written in the late twenties and early thirties, the years he spent in Europe. Even nearly sixty years later I could feel the solidarity of their love in those fragile, creased pages. Feeling like an intruder, I set this folder aside and opened the last.

The thinnest of the three, this envelope was so light it felt almost empty. Inside were three celluloid pouches, and in each of these was a lock of hair. A coil of the softest, blondest hair like spun sunlight, a curl of caramel-colored brown and a ringlet of taffy gold. Each lock was tied at one end with a faded-blue satin ribbon. My heart tightened as I realized what they represented...a lock of downy hair from the head of each new baby boy, lovingly preserved by their mother.

Walker, Arthur and Merton.

I didn't know which was my father's, so I held them all, in their celluloid envelopes, to my chest and waited for the pain to pass. Daddy. For the first time since I arrived, I felt his presence—a warm, gurgling baby; an irrepressible toddler, into everything; a delightful grade schooler, bringing his mother bouquets of wilted violets gripped too tightly between grubby fingers.

He had lived here, grown up here, bursting with life. The other boys, too. Merton and my father were the boisterous ones, I guessed, while Walker was more staid. I glanced around the cluttered study. Uncle Walker wrote his fairy stories here, seriously pursuing a frivolous subject. My gaze fell on the Maxfield Parrish magazine cover of the giant holding the prince in his palm, and I wondered why my uncle chose to hang that picture in the room he worked in every day. Was he the captive prince, or was the little figure one of his brothers?

Questions always seemed to lead to more questions, never answers.

I bundled the photograph album and the folder of love letters under one arm, deciding to look at the other things later. I also left behind one of my crutches. It was time to fly free, even with only one wing.

Out on the porch, the morning hummed with activity. Bees were busy in the honeysuckle. A robin launched itself off the porch railing, giving that warning cry that sounded like maniacal laughter. I could almost hear grass grow and new leaves unfurl, nature was that vigorous around this house.

Jinx swooped down as I settled on the glider, his black feathers glistening in the sun. He had an old pop top in his beak, the kind used on soft-drink cans years ago. He dropped the bit of aluminum in my lap and looked up at me, waiting for praise.

"Oh, isn't that wonderful! Just look at this beautiful pop top. Aren't you a fine bird!" I slipped the pop top on my finger like a ring. Jinx reached over and pulled it off. He wasn't a total sucker over a few flattering words.

He flew to a maple tree where he had a stash of pop tops stored in the deep crotch formed by three branches and added his latest to his treasure trove. Then he sat on a limb and muttered to himself the way he did when he was content.

I was dying to go through the picture album first, but forced myself to read at least parts of my grandparents' letters. Apparently they were newlyweds in 1928, when the letters began. The opening and closing sentences were blazing declarations of undying love, which I skipped, feeling more like a Peeping Tom than ever. Some reference was always made to the house. In my grandmother's letters to Seth, she talked about the renovations that were taking place in his absence. In Seth's letters to her, he usually mentioned a "surprise" he was sending her. After I caught on to the rhythm of the lover's private game, I located my grandmother's reply, thanking him for the lamp he picked up at an estate sale, which was perfect for the parlor or whatever.

I was looking for the most important trinket he sent to Isabelle while overseas—the brooch my father supposedly gave to Kathryn. From the collection of letters I learned that Seth came home occasionally, and after one of these visits, my grandmother wrote and shyly told him she was expecting their first child. Walker was born in June, 1935, while Seth was in Switzerland. The rumblings of war brought Seth home. Merton was born in 1942, and my father came along in 1944.

Through the letters, I was pretty much able to piece together my grandparents' lives. Even the gaps in communication were explained and missing events filled in. Except for one period. There were no letters for the year 1934 and no catch-up of events in the following year. It was as if that year had fallen through the cracks. Or else something so horrible had happened that neither wanted to acknowledge it in letters.

A niggling thought tugged at the edge of my conscious, like a sparrow pulling at a stubborn piece of string it wanted for its nest. Why didn't they write to each other that year...?

Zandra came out on the porch, slamming the screen door needlessly. "What's that junk?" she asked, indicating the folder and photo album.

It was on the tip of my tongue to say, "None of your business," and ask her what she was gussied up for. But on the other hand, since she was a Highsmith, too, it was her business, sort of. And I knew she had dressed with extra care hoping Victor Denton would show up this afternoon. His visits had tapered off and Zandra was barely fit to live with.

She plumped herself down next to me on the glider. Lately she had taken to wearing makeup, which enhanced her dark, gypsylike features. The bronze blusher she'd applied to her cheeks brought out chiseled hollows. Framed by mascaraed lashes, her tea-colored eyes looked even lighter than mine. If she'd lose that petulant pout, Alexandra Highsmith would be a stunner.

"What are you doing?" she asked in a tone that was more conversational than interested.

"Going through some old family papers," I replied, hastily shoving the love letters back into the folder.

"Still on your quest for the truth about the great family scandal?" She swung her legs around to tuck beneath her. "Ow!" she cried, pulling a bent pop top from under her thigh. "What the— Is this your idea of a joke, Holly? Booby-trapping the chair?"

"Not at all," I said, wanting to laugh. "It's a souvenir from Jinx. Or his calling card, however you want to look at it. He has a whole mess of them stuffed in that tree over there."

"That stupid bird. I wish he'd fly south or something." She rubbed the dent the sharp edge of the pop top had imprinted on her leg.

"I've been wondering...does Jinx fly south for the winter?"

"Are you kidding? He stays here winter and summer. Where else could he get mooch handouts?" She lifted the lid of the album. "Oh. Pictures. Can I see?"

I was surprised. "Haven't you seen these before?" Surely she must have...she'd lived in this house all her life.

"Once. A long time ago. But I forgot." She moved closer to me and put the heavy book across both our laps. If I hadn't been sitting down, I would have fainted. This was the first conciliatory gesture Zandra had made since I'd come here.

The album was artistically arranged—a photographic journey through the decades of our grandparents' lives. On the first two pages were portraits of Seth and Isabelle before their marriage. Isabelle wore bobbed hair and the short fringed dress of the flapper. Seth was snappy in baggy trousers and a straw hat. An engagement picture preceded several pages of wedding shots. Their wedding was elegant but not elaborate. The bride and groom had eyes only for each other, never the camera.

"Here's the house when Seth first bought it," Zandra commented, pointing to a blurred photo of a barely recognizable Blackbird Keep. The trees were smaller and the left wing had not been added yet, so the house had a half-finished appearance.

We flipped through shots of the house at various stages, while the wing was under reconstruction and the broken-down porch was being rebuilt. There were also picture postcards Seth had sent from Europe, but these had been pasted in the album, not hinged as the photographs were, so I couldn't lift them out to read Seth's messages on the backs.

I was anxious to get to the part when the boys were born. I couldn't wait to see baby pictures of my father. Mom didn't have a one, though she had a whole boxful of pictures of herself as a child and of my father after they were married. When I came along, Mom must have bitten the "brag book" bug that new mothers are susceptible to. She started a family album that we never looked at anymore because it was still painful to watch the progression of our family from three to two.

Zandra turned a page. "Here's Dad. Look at all that hair! You'd never know to look at him now." Baby Walker squinted at the camera from an old-fashioned baby carriage. His hair sprouted all over his head in adorable curls. There was another picture of Walker in his high chair, an unsmiling toddler soberly holding a tin cup as if he were expected to propose an impromptu toast before an assembly of judges.

"Cute," I said, mainly because it seemed the thing to say. Actually, Zandra looked remarkably like her father right now as she squinted to see the picture better. All she needed was a tin cup.

I skipped several pages, anxiety knotting my stomach, knowing what I would find as if I were experiencing a flash of déjà vu. Chronologically, pictures of Merton and Arthur should have followed.

But the pages were blank. Hinges forming snapshot-sized rectangles outlined where the pictures had been. My grandmother's careful script spelled out both Merton's and Arthur's names like captions describing phantoms.

I flipped through the album frantically. No trace of either son. Their pictures had been methodically, almost surgically removed from the family album as if they had ceased to exist. The empty pages stared back at me with time-worn blandness, the way the scar from a pruned tree branch eventually heals over.

Chapter Eight

Here I am—ready to kidnap the two prettiest girls in Delaware and take them to lunch!" Victor proclaimed as he got out of his car. "How does the Ice-House Café sound?"

"Cool," Zandra said, uncurling from the glider as gracefully as her cat, who lay under the chaise like a drugged panther.

July ushered in another endless heat wave that made us indolent as alligators. Even lifting a glass of lemonade required more effort than reversing the gravity field. Because Blackbird Keep wasn't air conditioned, we all sat around like zombies during the day, coming to life only in the evenings when the tiniest of breezes cut through the humid, stale air.

Victor clapped his hands together to rouse us. That day he was wearing slate-gray slacks and a short-sleeved shirt that was still crisp. I didn't know how he always managed to look so unruffled. Didn't he sweat like the rest of the world?

"Come on, you two. Up and at 'em. I said I'd be here at eleven-thirty."

I peeled my sticky back from the wicker chair. "Not to me, you didn't. What's this about lunch? Zandra?"

"I thought you'd go with Mom and Dad today," she said, unconcerned. "You acted interested last night."

"Only because I figured the drive into Pennsylvania might be nice. Couldn't you see me in all those itty-bitty antique places—the proverbial bull in the china shop. But when I begged off, you could have told me then about Victor taking us to lunch."

"It must have slipped my mind."

I was mad, which only served to make me hotter. Zandra had taken a shower not a half an hour ago, emerging in a new sundress and reeking of Jean Naté, refreshed as a native in *South Pacific*. She had known all along that Victor was coming to take us to lunch and she never breathed a word. I guess she hoped I'd back out, since I wasn't ready. Well, I'd show her I wasn't that easily discouraged.

Putting down the old household-account book I was studying, I struggled to my feet. "Be right with you guys. Don't leave without me!"

In the guest room, I stood before the deep, cedar-lined closet. What could I wear to accessorize Basic Cast? I had brought only two semidecent skirts, and they were both in the dirty laundry. Dressed in my underwear, I hung on the door, petrified with indecision. I probably looked like a painting done by one of the Old Masters—*Girl Standing Before Closet (Trying To Make Up Her Mind)*.

There was only the sherbet-striped jumper I had worn the day Kyle took me to visit his Aunt Kathryn. I remembered putting it on that morning, certain Kyle would notice me in something pretty for a change. He hadn't. Even if I had worn a beaded evening gown and feather boa, all he would have noticed was how like my grandfather I was.

Maybe Victor Denton would appreciate me in pastel cotton. Feeling slightly disloyal, I pulled the jumper over the one clean blouse I had left, slicked a little raspberry gloss over my lips, brushed my hair, then joined the others on the porch in less than five minutes. Never let it be said I held up anybody's lunch.

One corner of Zandra's mouth twisted when she saw me. She'd probably been praying I'd break my other leg on the way downstairs.

"I'll be the envy of Draper's Heights," Victor said. "Escorting two beautiful girls to lunch." He crooked his arms at right angles to his body. "Do you like chicken?" he asked us. When we both nodded, he said, "Well, take a wing!"

Located on a side street near the library, the Ice-House Café was exactly what it sounded like—an old ice-storage building that had been converted into a restaurant. The rough-board walls had been painted a muted blue-green and unattractive overhead pipes were camouflaged with hanging ferns. Daguerreotypes of men in handlebar mustaches and old photographs of the place when it was in its ice-packing heyday adorned the walls. An assortment of the huge ice tongs brawny men used to carry blocks of ice to the customers' iceboxes with were suspended over the copper-flashed bar.

The waiter, who wore Gay Nineties sleeve garters, led us to the table Victor had reserved, away from the juke box but near the bricked-in grill where vegetables and seafood were cooked to order.

"What's the occasion?" I asked Victor when we were seated. "Did you win the Pulitzer or something?"

He laughed. "Not hardly. I just thought it would be a special treat. I'm forever at your place, swilling Gray's lemonade, scarfing her cookies."

"Mom loves having you come over," Zandra assured him.

"Well, the feeling is mutual. Your parents are fascinating people. And that big, old house is so wonderful." He hesitated a moment. "I actually called Gray last week to set up a lunch date for all of us. But she told me of her and your father's plans to go on an antique junket and asked if I minded taking you girls. Would I mind, I told her? Does the sun rise in the east?"

How could he do this, I wondered, perusing the menu. Didn't Victor realize Zandra was crazy about him? And what about me? It was always understood that I was first on his list. At least I *thought* I was. So why take two feuding female cousins to lunch? Did he enjoy indigestion? I knew Zandra was going to try her best to make me look bad in front of him.

I didn't have to wait long. After we ordered, the three of us chatted about inconsequential matters—the heat, the Oriole's last game, a TV miniseries that had bombed. But the minute the waiter brought our food, Zandra started sniping at me.

"Holly, have you seen Kyle lately?" she asked innocently.

I stared at the vegetable tempura arranged on my plate, as if looking for the answer under a slice of zucchini. "Not lately," I mumbled.

"Who's Kyle?" Victor inquired.

"Kyle Thompkins. This guy Holly met in town. She met him outside the Safeway."

"No, I didn't," I set her straight. "I met him before then. The first time I came into town."

Victor paused, a forkful of pasta halfway to his mouth. "That was the day I saw you in the drugstore, wasn't it?"

I squirmed in my seat, pretending to adjust my cast. "I guess so. Pass the pepper, please."

As Zandra handed me the pepper mill, she had her next dart ready to throw. "So where did you two disappear to last week? Daddy says you were awfully mysterious about it."

Forgetting Victor was sitting across from me, I said, "How did you know we went out?" And why dredge this up now, I felt like hurling back. Kyle had taken me to Kathryn's days ago. I was learning the hard way that Zandra liked to save up ammunition to use when it suited her purpose. Like now.

"I saw you leave from my window. Do you really think you can keep something like that a secret?"

The tempura was heavenly—strips of carrots and broccoli and zucchini breaded in an ice-water batter and deep-fried so crispy and light I half expected my plate to float over the table. But I might have been eating sawdust, the way I felt. No one could find out about my visit to Kathryn—I didn't want to cause the poor woman any more pain. Kyle had told me she kept to herself, seldom going into town. Her shyness made her vulnerable to idle gossip.

I had to make up an excuse. Anything to throw Zandra off the scent. "We went—" I sifted through the places Kyle mentioned he liked "—we went to...Bombay Hook!"

"Bombay Hook? All the way over there?" Zandra frowned. "You weren't really gone that long."

"Yeah, well, we didn't stay," I amended lamely.

"It's a nice drive over in that direction," Victor said.

"Yes, it is." I could have kissed him.

Zandra turned back to her quiche, obviously disappointed Victor hadn't acted more agitated over my date with Kyle. But she wasn't about to fall back and retreat. "Did Holly tell you the mission she's on while she's staying here?"

"What mission?" Victor glanced at me, more interested in this than a potential rival.

"Shall I tell him, Holly? Or do you want to?"

"I wouldn't dream of depriving you of the pleasure," I replied, my tone acid enough to tarnish the copper railing that sectioned the tables into intimate groupings.

"Holly is trying to clear her father's name." Zandra made me sound like a cross between Mary Poppins and Mother Teresa.

Victor reached over and harpooned an onion ring off my plate. "Since you're not going to eat it. What terrible thing did your father do, Holly?" He knew my father was dead—we had swapped vital statistics during our first meeting.

I hated Zandra's bringing up a subject this sensitive in a public restaurant. Discussing my father's situation over quiche and pasta seemed to trivialize it somehow. "He fell in love with a girl from the village. He and my grandfather didn't see eye-to-eye on things, so my dad left home. For good. He never came back."

"Because of this girl?" Victor prompted.

"Holly didn't tell the whole story," Zandra put in. "Her father gave a family heirloom to this girl and that made my grandfather mad. She also left out the fact that her father and his brother—my Uncle Merton, not my father—were both in love with this girl at the same time."

"We don't know if Daddy gave Ka—the girl the brooch. Just because Seth said it, doesn't make it so," I said hotly.

"Seth was your grandfather. The one who trained birds," Victor said.

I nodded.

"What was the family heirloom your father allegedly gave to his girlfriend?"

"A brooch," I replied. "Not valuable. At least not in dollars. My grandfather sent it to my grandmother when he was in Europe, so I guess it had sentimental value."

"Are you sure?" Victor stopped eating, his interest fully engaged. "Your grandfather may have thought he was picking up a little trinket for your grandmother, when in reality it could be something worth a lot of money today."

I looked at Zandra. She shook her head slightly and said, "Most of the stuff my grandfather sent back from overseas was furniture. Nothing to get excited about."

"That Chippendale chair in the hall isn't exactly a Woolworth's special," Victor disputed.

"Oh, that." Zandra flipped a hand. "It's just a chair."

"See what I mean? You've grown up surrounded with those things. You don't see their worth because you've lived with all those chairs and tables and lamps and pictures. Not seen them roped off in a museum the way the rest of us have."

He had a point. Zandra didn't realize the value of the presents Seth had sent to his wife because they were always part of her home. And I didn't realize the value because of sheer ignorance. A Chippendale chair could have bitten me on the leg and I wouldn't have known the difference.

I leaned toward Victor. "So you're saying that this brooch could be worth a lot of money and that's why Seth made such a big deal over it when he thought my father gave it away."

"Possibly." Victor folded his napkin and laid it beside his plate. "Do you have any diaries or letters your grandparents wrote? Any old papers?"

"Aunt Gray found some things for me to go through. But so far I haven't had much luck," I replied. "A household account book, some business letters and some...love letters." I deliberately left out the photo album, silently daring Zandra to bring it up. The shock of learning that my father's pictures had been excised like a bad tooth was still too raw.

"Love letters," Victor mused aloud. "Between your grandparents, I assume. And you didn't find any clues in them?"

"I read about the other stuff Seth sent back from Europe, but not a syllable about any brooch." The lack of letters for the year 1934 flashed through my brain, but before I could hold on to that thought Victor asked me something else.

"What about the business letters? Did you go through those?"

I shook my head. "Too dull. I couldn't plow through them."

"This is most intriguing," Victor said in a poor imitation of Cary Grant. "An honest-to-goodness mystery in our sleepy little town. We simply must pursue it. Tell you what," he went on in his normal voice. "When we get back to your place, we'll all sit down and read those business letters. Maybe something will turn up." He smiled at us both. "Dessert, ladies? I hear the vanilla-mousse pie is a real killer."

I'll say this for Victor Denton. His powers of organization are truly awesome. In no time, the three of us were sitting on the floor in the recreation area of the kitchen, piles of letters divided between us.

"Don't waste time reading the whole letter," he instructed. "Skim for the gist of what the letter is about. We're looking for some activity your grandfather was involved in that would have put him in contact with the brooch or the person who sold him the brooch."

The letters were even more boring than I remembered. Whatever business Seth conducted overseas completely escaped me. I couldn't fathom a word of what I was reading. Facing up to this shortcoming was a good lesson, though. I resolved to apply myself to my classes more diligently next year, knowing that if I was forced to look for work as a secretary instead of attending college on a scholarship, I'd flub my first interview.

Zandra sagged against the trunk and fanned herself with a stack of unread letters. "This is a total bore. Even if we find out the brooch was one of the crown jewels, what good would it do? It's gone and it's been gone since Holly's father gave it to that girl."

I glowered at her. "I wish you'd stop saying that. And what makes you so sure it was my father? It could have been Merton, you know. Maybe he hid it so my father would get in trouble with Seth. Remember, they loved the same girl. He had good cause."

"Maybe," Zandra conceded. "But I doubt it. If all Seth cared about was getting the brooch back, he wouldn't have accused your father unless he believed he took it. If he thought Merton stole it, he would have blamed him."

"Conjecture is all well and good, but it doesn't help us find reference to that brooch," Victor chided us, his face so stern I actually thought he meant it for a second. "Zandra, get back to the letters."

I was on my third pile of heretofores and whereases when a sentence leaped out at me. "Victor, look at this. Does this mean anything?"

He snatched the letter from my hand. "Where?"

"Right below the part about shipping the order on time."

His face changed as he read the paragraph. Then he looked at me with the same expression of triumph he gave me in the toy room on his first unannounced visit to Blackbird Keep. "Give the little lady a cigar," he drawled.

"Did I find something?" I couldn't believe it.

"You sure did."

Zandra scooted over. "What? Show me." After reading the letter, she was still puzzled. "What does it mean? So he met some old Russian guy. Big deal. What's that got to do with the brooch?" I could tell she hated being the only one in the dark. I didn't understand what the letter meant, either, only that Seth's reference to dinner with a Russian gentleman struck me somehow.

Victor got up and helped himself to a diet soda from the refrigerator. He found the cupboard where the glasses were kept with such familiarity it was hard for me to keep in mind he had only been in the house a handful of times.

"Have either of you ever heard of the Romanovs? The Imperial family of Russia? Or Fabergé?"

"No," I replied. Zandra shook her head.

"Don't tell me you don't know anything about the Russian Revolution?" He pretended to be stunned. "What are they teaching you children these days?"

"I take world history next year," I said tartly. "In the meantime, why don't you just spit it out?"

"All right. I'll make it short and simple." He took a large swallow of his soda. "Lenin, who was the leader of the Bolsheviks, overthrew the Imperial government in Russia in—let me see, 1917 or 1918, I forget which. The ruler at the time was Czar Nicholas. He abdicated the throne and was later executed. The whole Romanov dynasty had to flee Russia or else face the same consequences.'' His information-trained mind spewed out facts like a computer.

"What's this got to do with the man Seth mentions in his letter?'' I asked, impatient to get the connection to the brooch.

Victor smacked the letter with the flat of his palm. "The 'old Russian guy,' as Zandra so aptly calls him, claimed to be a member of the Imperial court. Your grandfather met him while in Switzerland.''

"But the letter was dated 1934,'' Zandra said. "All that stuff happened back in 1918.''

I stared at her. 1934. She picked up on the date and I never noticed. That was the year Seth and Isabelle didn't write each other. Or else someone came along later and destroyed the letters for that period. The same person who removed my father's and Merton's pictures from the album?

Victor's voice pulled my attention back to the present. "... could have gone underground all those years. By the time Seth met him, he felt secure enough to reveal his secret. Or maybe he was sick of hiding out. Or homesick. By the thirties the Communist regime was well established, so there was never any hope of returning to Russia.''

"How does all this tie in with the brooch?'' I pressed.

"You didn't give me a chance to finish,'' Victor said reproachfully. "In the days of Nicholas life was very grand for the Romanovs. They were ridiculously rich. So rich, that ordinary jewels meant nothing to them. A very famous man named Fabergé made fabulous jeweled Easter eggs for the Imperial family. They were fantastic creations—you'd have to see them to fully appreciate what I mean. I saw a show at the Cooper-Hewitt Museum in New York a few years ago, so I know what I'm talking about. One egg had a solid gold miniature coach inside, every detail perfect. Another had an orange tree inside, with a tiny little bird that sang.''

My brain waves finally clicked with his. "You think this Russian guy was a member of royalty and he met my grandfather and sold him one of these eggs.''

"Probably not an egg,'' Victor qualified. "There were only a set number of those eggs ever made and most have been accounted for. But Fabergé made other things, too. Cigarette cases, rings, necklaces . . . and brooches. All very rare—and all priceless.''

The enormity of the situation finally hit. When I spoke my voice was as serious as a banker's. ''Then the brooch could be worth a lot of money? You weren't far off when you said it might be a crown jewel,'' I added to Zandra.

Apparently she was as flabbergasted as I was. ''I was only kidding. If the thing was worth so much, why didn't Seth tell anybody?''

Victor shrugged. ''Who knows? He was a funny old coot, wasn't he? He must have been to fool around with crows. Obviously his elevator didn't go all the way to the top.'' He stared at my cousin, his eyes dilating slightly, as if an idea had suddenly occurred to him. ''Maybe he wasn't so crazy, after all. He *did* leave a clue.''

''What?'' Zandra asked. ''This letter?''

''That and one other thing.'' Victor gave a smug, self-satisfied smile, as if he'd discovered the formula for recycling garbage into greenbacks and he wasn't going to let anyone else in on it.

''Come on!'' Zandra threw a candle-wicked pillow at him. ''Tell!''

''Your name,'' he said. ''Alexandra. I'll bet your grandfather had some influence on what your parents decided to name you.''

''I don't know. Even if he did, I still don't get it.'' I was just as bewildered as she was.

''The Czarina of Imperial Russia,'' Victor said expansively, ''Nicholas's wife was named Alexandra.''

I nearly tripped over it, stumbling down the dimly lit hall after supper later that night.

The jester lay next to the toy room, grinning stiff-necked at the ceiling. My skin crawled at the thought of touching the loathsome thing, but I couldn't leave it lying on the floor, a potential safety hazard. What was the doll doing there, anyway? Why wasn't it in the elephant-leg umbrella stand where it belonged? Uncle Walker would have a fit if he saw his jester on the floor.

I picked it up by its stick so that mocking face was turned away from me. That was when I noticed the toy-room door was ajar.

"Uncle Walker? Aunt Gray? Are you in there?" I knew they weren't. They were sitting on the porch not fifteen feet away, trying to cool off though the temperature was still in the eighties. Zandra must be inside. I pushed the door open and looked around, but there was no sign of my cousin, either.

This was very strange. First the jester on the floor and now the toy-room door open again with no one inside. I knew how very particular my uncle was about his collection. He just didn't forget to lock the door. Maybe Zandra had. She had used the hidden key once. But knowing how strict her father was, why would she leave the door open? To irritate him?

I didn't want to step over that threshold. But as before, I was drawn into the room, as if my grandfather were summoning me with the power of the last Imperial Czar Victor told us about and I couldn't disobey.

"What do you want?" I whispered, feeling his strength wrap around me like a coronation robe. Dead or not, Seth Highsmith still ruled Blackbird Keep, at least in this room. Why was I the object of his venom? Was this a test to see if I was truly worthy of the name Highsmith?

Then I sensed someone was watching me, just as before. But this time I was able to separate Seth's vibes from the prying eyes. It wasn't my grandfather's spirit glaring at me, I was certain. No, this was yet another unseen enemy.

The room suddenly filled with light. Uncle Walker came in, his face thunderous upon discovering me there.

"Holly? What are you doing?" All I could think was how little resemblance he bore to the pudgy-cheeked baby in the photo album.

"I—saw the door was open and I came—"

"This door is locked at all times!" He swatted my explanation away like an annoying wasp. "It couldn't have been open."

"But it was! And I found this on the floor just outside." I held the jester up as proof.

He strode over and took it away from me. "On the floor? My Parrish jester? Impossible. Holly, I know you're a guest with us this summer, but you know the rules. The toy room is off-limits. Even Gray doesn't come in here to dust without asking me first."

"But Zandra said she could go in anytime! She even knows where—"

He cut me off before I could tell him about the time his daughter gave Victor and me an unauthorized tour of the collection room.

"No one is allowed in here without my permission. I don't know what's going on here, but I intend to get to the bottom of this." He scanned the shelves, apparently checking to see that his dolls and toys weren't upset by my intrusion.

"Oh, no!" he cried.

"What is it?" I began to quiver as his panic was transmitted to me.

"My Rapunzel marionette. She's gone!"

Chapter Nine

Nobody came right out and said it, but I knew they all thought I was involved with the missing marionette. Uncle Walker made me recount at least four times how I came upon the jester lying on the floor and then found the open door.

If I hadn't brought it up, I don't think Zandra would have ever confessed she knew the whereabouts of the hidden key. But after I cornered her by telling Uncle Walker about the time she showed the toy room to Victor, she grudgingly admitted she had used the extra key on occasion. But not recently. And certainly not that night.

Which swung the finger of guilt back around to me. Accusation, even by implication, tends to make one desperate.

"Maybe Victor found the key and went in," I said, grasping at straws. "He was here for a while after he brought us back from lunch." Uncle Walker was already checking to see if the key was in its usual place under the umbrella stand.

"And stole the Rapunzel doll?" Aunt Gray was incredulous. "Never. Not that sweet boy."

That "sweet boy" had a mind like a steel trap, I had discovered this afternoon when we went through my grandfather's business letters. Victor was onto something with the link to the Russian court jewels, I was certain. And I was equally certain I would never have made the association, even if Seth had drawn a treasure map on the back of that letter with "X marks the spot" in letters five-inches high.

Uncle Walker came back, shaking his head. "The key is still there. Whoever broke into the toy room wouldn't have gone to all the trouble of putting the key back and then left the door open. A burglar would have kept the key or thrown it away. And stolen more, while he was at it." He bent to examine the lock on the heavy paneled door. "No sign of forced entry." Now he sounded like one of those police-procedural shows on TV. "You know the strangest thing of all? I tested the lock on my way in to dinner, out of habit. Rapunzel was stolen between supper and just now. Victor Denton was long gone by then. So that lets him off the hook."

But not me, I could read in his eyes, tea-colored like mine but narrowed with suspicion. I mumbled something about being tired and dragged myself upstairs to bed. I could hear Aunt Gray worriedly suggesting they ought to report the incident.

I *was* tired. Sick and tired of Blackbird Keep, with its endless riddles and hostile inhabitants. Despite the fact that I wanted to exonerate my father and learn more about his past, this house continued to turn on me. I was a Highsmith in name and eye color only, as far as these unforgiving walls were concerned. If I lived here until the stone chimneys crumbled to dust, I would still be treated like an intruder.

When I had changed into the short dorm shirt I wore to bed, I clumped over to the windows. Below, the garden was still and muted, as if all vibrancy had drained with the setting sun. Somewhere a cardinal gave a halfhearted cheer, cheer, cheer. Dusk these days was endless—the sky changed hues so gradually, I had the feeling the secret of life was being revealed in those shifting shades of lilac and mint green. If only I had the special glasses one needed to read the message.

The woman in white—Kyle's Aunt Kathryn—didn't haunt the garden this evening. I wondered if those twilight searches were unconsciously acted out on her part. I think Kyle would have known if she purposefully walked to Blackbird Keep from town just to wander through the tangled weeds looking for the missing brooch. I'm sure he'd watch her more carefully if he knew. The next time I saw him, I vowed to tell him, before Aunt Kathryn got hurt. Seth's menacing spirit could envelope her, as it had done to me in the toy room earlier. His evilness was not contained within the bounds of Uncle Walker's collection of dolls and puppets. I could feel his influence seeping into the rest of the house like the noxious fumes of carbon monoxide—present, but undetected until it's too late.

"Daddy," I whispered. "Was it this horrible for you, too?" No wonder he left and never came back. When my sentence of exile was up, I'd never come back, either.

The missing marionette cast a pall over the whole house, spoiling everyday routines the way a milk ring from a sticky glass mars the surface of a priceless coffee table.

When I passed the toy room on my way to breakfast the next day, I saw Uncle Walker in there with clipboard and pen, frantically taking inventory to make sure nothing else had disappeared. He didn't look up when I waved from the doorway, so I knew which list I was on.

"Aunt Gray," I appealed to her, "I hope he doesn't think I stole that doll, because I didn't. I don't take things that don't belong to me. I never have."

She patted me reassuringly on the arm. "Of course you didn't, Holly. But the doll *is* gone. *Somebody* took it. I suppose it might have been a very clever tramp. You read about all kinds of things going on in the paper these days. People don't think isolated houses are broken into much, but they are."

"If a tramp had broken in, wouldn't he have taken more than just one puppet, as Uncle Walker said last night?" Her logic was off-center, though I was glad to have an ally.

"I don't know," she said honestly. "If I had my way, those ghastly dolls and jesters would be in a museum somewhere. But Walker's passion for old toys is harmless, so I shouldn't complain. As gruesome as they are, toys are silent at least, which is more than I can say for those pesky blackbirds Seth trained. When Jinx goes, this house will be peaceful at last."

When Jinx passed on to that Great Cuttlebone in the sky, she meant. I wondered what the life span of the average crow was—not that Jinx was your average crow by any stretch of the imagination. One of the books Aunt Gray located for us to go through was Seth's research on his birds. I resolved to start reading it after supper—that is, if Uncle Walker didn't have me on bread and water by then.

The rest of the day we all tiptoed around Uncle Walker, who, in his despair over his missing Rapunzel, was unable to work on his book. It was as though a beloved member of the family had died. "He'll get over it," Aunt Gray predicted in a voice so low and grave she could have been a receptionist in a funeral parlor. "Things will be better tomorrow."

They weren't. By comparison, a mortuary was more laughs than Blackbird Keep.

My only reprieve came when Aunt Gray reminded me that I had an appointment at the medical center to have my cast taken off at long last. My records and X rays had been transferred from my regular doctor in Indiana to an orthopedic specialist, so everything was in order.

Zandra drove us into town, vanishing practically the instant she switched off the Daimler's engine.

"Aren't you coming with us to the doctor?" her mother called after her.

"No. Meet you here in a little while," Zandra threw back over her shoulder. I noted her direction—uptown toward the newspaper office. Was she going to see Victor?

I was so anxious to get my cast off I didn't even flinch when the doctor brandished his electric saw. The cast came off neatly, like a split coconut shell, exposing my withered, lily-white leg covered with fine black hair.

"It looks terrible!" I exclaimed. "Are you sure it's all right?"

"It *does* look terrible," the doctor agreed, which did little to instill confidence in me. I craned my neck to check out his framed medical degrees hanging on the wall. "Of course, it's been wrapped up away from sunlight for many weeks, while your good leg has been hopping around, getting a tan."

Testily I flexed my knee, straightening my leg. That worked, at least. "But it looks all shriveled, as if I had polio or something."

"Your muscles have shrunk. That 'shriveled' look, as you put it, will go away as you strengthen those muscles. You won't be able to walk on this leg right off.'' He poked and prodded a few minutes more, then released me, wanting to see me again before I went back home.

I had thought I could throw down my crutches forever, like one of those people miraculously cured by a faith healer, but I stumped out of the clinic with the hateful things wedged under my arms, as usual. The fresh air felt funny on my leg, which looked funny, too. The hair had grown inside the cast, and my shin was so furry I was mortified to be seen in public.

"While I'm in town, I'd like to do a little shopping," Aunt Gray said. She looked at my leg, dead white like a prisoner just released after ten years in a windowless cell. One that left prison wearing a skimpy fur coat, that is. "What about you, Holly? Are you all right? Do you want to go rest in the car until Zandra comes back? Or do you want to go home and lie down?"

"I'll be fine," I told her, having just spotted Ed's Garage across the street. "My leg doesn't bother me a bit. You run along and take your time."

Pale, hairy leg or no, I couldn't miss an opportunity to speak to Kyle Thompkins. Inside the garage, I swung my crutches between coils of air hoses and stacks of dead tires with the agility of Tarzan. A man who looked like an Ed, despite the fact that the name stitched on his shirt pocket read Perry, told me I'd find Kyle out in one of the back bays. I crossed a courtyard dotted with ailing cars to a second, smaller garage.

Kyle was in the first wide-open doorway, which I guessed was a bay. The top half of him was hidden under a burgundy Ford Ranger, but I recognized those California-slim legs encased in oil-stained jeans.

"Hi, there," I greeted him. "Anybody home?"

He slid out on the low-wheeled mechanic's creeper. "Holly," he said, surprised. "You got your cast off! How does your leg feel?"

Wouldn't you know he'd zero in on my least desirable body part? "It's okay. A little weak, but the doctor said that'd go away. How come I haven't heard from you lately?"

He stood, wiping his hands on a greasy rag that dangled from a belt loop. "I couldn't call you—not there."

"Well, I couldn't very well call *you*. I don't know your number or where you live or anything," I returned defensively. Why did Kyle twist every conversation, no matter how simple, into a wrestling match? Would we always square off whenever we met like the Hatfields and the McCoys?

"To tell you the truth," he said, running his fingers through his thick, Beach Boy bangs, "I've been avoiding you."

"No kidding."

"Look, Holly. I've nothing against you personally—"

"Just my father and my grandfather and a few dozen other ancestors with the same last name," I put in sharply.

"But I was really shook when I saw the effect you had on Aunt Kathryn," he finished. "For her sake—and yours—I think we'd better forget this brooch business."

I wanted to beat him over the head with one of my crutches. He was so dense! "If we forget about it, then your aunt will be tormented by guilt the rest of her days. She's already obsessed with finding the pin."

He stared at me. "What do you mean?"

"I saw her wandering the grounds near the old aviary one night. From my window. She looked really out of it. As though she wasn't sure why she was there."

"Oh, Lord," he groaned. "What was she doing?"

"Poking through the weeds. Looking for something."

"The pin," he concluded. "Gosh, Holly. If Walker Highsmith saw her on his property, he'd have her arrested, you know. He thinks she's—well, not all there."

I hastened to put his mind at ease. "I've seen her only once, Kyle. And when I went to get someone, she was gone. And I know she got home safely, because you took me to see her."

His indigo eyes darkened, even in the gloom of the garage. "You mean, you saw Kathryn wandering around before that day and you never told me about it? Why?"

"I didn't realize it was her. The woman I saw in the garden wore a white dress. And she looked like an old lady at that distance. Even when I first met your aunt, I didn't make the connection. Not until the end . . . when she told us how my father showed her the brooch in the yard one time, remember? Then I figured she was the lady in white."

"That still doesn't answer my question," Kyle accused. "You had plenty of time to tell me going home that day."

I shook my head helplessly. "I couldn't. No, wait, don't get mad. I—things had gone so badly at your aunt's, I didn't want to worry you anymore."

"So why tell me now? Why bother at all? That's what I don't like about your family, Holly. Too many secrets. You can't trust a Highsmith as far as you can throw him. Or her."

"If that's the way you feel," I said coldly, "Then there's no point in continuing this discussion. I pity you, Kyle Thompkins. You've got such a chip on your shoulder, you'll never get anywhere in this world." I turned to leave, but couldn't resist adding, "For your information, I came over here to let you know what I've found out about the brooch. But since you're clearly not interested, I won't waste another second of your precious time."

I made the mistake of trying to stomp away, forgetting my cast was gone and in too big of a hurry to use my crutches. Slamming my full weight on my left leg for the first time in so many weeks caused my knee to buckle and give way. I would have fallen into a basin of murky oil if Kyle hadn't caught me around the waist with one strong arm.

"Sit down over here," he said, half carrying me to a dilapidated chair next to the soft-drink machine. "Every time I see you, Holly, you're always doing something stupid. If you're not drowning yourself in a fountain, you're trying to create a dryland oil spill." In a more concerned voice he said, "Are you okay? Does your leg hurt much?"

My leg was killing me, but not half as much as my wounded pride. He was right—I *was* suddenly Miss Klutzy whenever Kyle was around.

"I'm fine," I said as crisply as I could manage. "It was stupid, putting my weight on my leg like that. But I'm okay now."

"Look," he said. "I don't want you to leave in a huff. I have a break coming up. Suppose we go to the coffee shop on the corner and have a bite to eat. Do you have a schedule to keep?"

"No. Aunt Gray was going shopping. And Zandra took off for parts unknown. I have time."

"Good. Then let's go." He flashed his most winning grin and helped me to my feet.

It occurred to me then that Kyle Thompkins had a responsibility complex. He was defensive as long as he felt I was strong enough to take his opposition. But the minute I revealed a weaker side—as when my leg gave out—he reverted to his natural, caring self. This is the Kyle I was attracted to in the beginning, the Kyle who protected his vulnerable aunt and visited wildlife refuges alone. He would help a sparrow with an injured wing, but would have little sympathy for a blue jay that robbed other birds' nests. He hated bullies. No wonder he despised my grandfather, even in death.

Now if I had been smart, I would have played up to this nurturing side of his. Let him think my leg hurt more than it really did. Use it to cuddle up to him. But, then, I've never been noted for doing the smart thing. As soon as I was able, I stalked out of the garage ahead of him, independent as ever.

The coffee shop on the corner was so nondescript and coffee-shopish it was nearly invisible. We sat down on a regular-issue vinyl-covered table with the requisite uneven legs, so that when Kyle leaned his elbows on the table across from me, I had to lean on mine to keep the table from rocking. I ordered the same as Kyle, black coffee and a grilled cheese, feeling like a character in a badly directed Bogart movie.

"We are always starting off on the wrong foot," Kyle acknowledged.

"Maybe it's because of my bum leg," I teased.

His face was earnest. "I don't want it to be this way."

"Then let's talk like two normal people. I'll begin. How are you, Kyle? Now you're supposed to say, 'Fine, Holly. And how are *you*?' And so on, until we're carrying on a real conversation, not arguing. Got it?"

"It won't work, Holly," he said with a sigh. "We're not any two normal people. We're practically related, if not in fact, then by what your father did to my aunt twenty-five years ago."

I had to agree. "It's not fair—because of them, we're affected, even after all this time. But if we clear up that mess about the missing brooch, then we'll be free to be friends. Or whatever. Right?" I looked at him hopefully.

Our food came then—charcoaled cheese sandwiches and coffee so black and murky I was sure the waitress had run back to Ed's Garage and dipped our cups in the pan of oil I nearly toppled.

Kyle sipped his without wincing, so I guessed it was safe to drink. But he didn't answer my last question. Instead he said, "You mentioned you found out something. What is it?"

I scraped toast ashes onto my plate while I told Kyle about the letter. His eyes widened when I got to the part about the Russian Seth met in Switzerland and Victor's conclusion regarding the Fabergé jewels that disappeared with the Imperial family.

"Who is this Victor?" he wanted to know.

"He works for the newspaper. You mean, you haven't heard of him? I thought everybody knew everybody in a town this small." I had little cause to act superior—I didn't know every single person in Miller's Forks and it was even smaller than Draper's Heights.

"Before you start rehearsing for the role of Emily in *Our Town*," Kyle said dryly, "let me remind you that people move in and out of here all the time. I don't really keep track."

"That's not what you told me the first time I saw you."

"What did I say?"

"You handed me some line about this town not being big enough to hide a new face." Actually, he had said "pretty" face, but I didn't want him to think I memorized every word that passed his lips.

"Oh, yeah?" Kyle looked a trifle embarrassed. "Well, that's what it was. A line."

I maneuvered the discussion back to the subject at hand. "Do you think Victor's theory holds water? That the pin was valuable and Seth knew it the whole time?"

"It makes sense. Maybe that's why he kept badgering Aunt Kathryn to return it. What else do you know about that jeweler—what was his name?"

"Fabergé," I supplied. "Nothing, besides what Victor told us. And I won't take his word for it, though he hasn't any reason to lie. First chance I get, I'm going to the library and look up this Fabergé guy."

Kyle was scribbling something on his napkin. "If you see Aunt Kathryn wandering around the garden again, give me a call and I'll come get her." He shoved the napkin across to me. There were two phone numbers on it. "The top one is my home number," he explained. "And the other is Ed's Garage.

Promise me you'll call? I don't want anything to happen to her. It's a long walk from town to your house.''

I tucked the napkin in the pocket of my skirt. "I promise. I don't want anything to happen to her, either, Kyle. I like your aunt. A lot.'' And I like you, too, I wanted to add.

"I know you do,'' he said, and for a moment I thought he had read my mind. "Outside of me and my mom, you're the only person who really understands her. I appreciate that.''

"I'm surprised Jinx hasn't dive-bombed her,'' I said lightly. "The welcoming committee at Blackbird Keep leaves much to be desired. When he attacked me that first day, I nearly died!''

"This is the crow your grandfather trained? I've always wanted to see that bird—he's famous in town, you know. He stays outdoors?'' Kyle asked.

I nodded. "Uncle Walker can't stand him. They have this ongoing feud because Jinx chews the morning paper and Uncle Walker won't let him in the house. I think that's Jinx's way of retaliating, but Uncle Walker won't give him credit for having a mind that's devious.''

"It's a shame the bird is left on its own.'' Kyle frowned. "That's the problem with taming wild animals—the person has to take full responsibility for its entire existence. Otherwise the animal is caught in some half world—it isn't wild and it isn't tame.''

"I'm sure my grandfather took very good care of Jinx when he was alive,'' I said. "Zandra says Seth got along better with his birds than he did with people.''

"I can believe it.''

The coffee-shop door opened and in came Zandra and Victor.

"Speak of the devil,'' I whispered to Kyle. "That's Victor Denton—the one I told you about.''

Except for Kyle and me, the restaurant was empty. Yet Victor steered Zandra to a table ludicrously far away, as though we had the plague. Zandra gave me a little salute as if to say, "He's mine now!'' and sat down. They bent their heads together and began talking in low tones.

I stared at Kyle. "Now what do you suppose has gotten into them?''

He shrugged. "Who knows? Maybe Denton doesn't like sharing."

I gulped the last bitter swallow of coffee uneasily. Kyle was half right. Maybe Victor wasn't thrilled sharing *me* with another guy. Maybe he took Zandra all the way over there to make me jealous. If I didn't like Kyle so much, I might have been. Zandra looked wonderful. Her hair shimmered down her back in a raven waterfall and she had on a new Indian cotton skirt and blouse. Bangle bracelets glinted at her wrist as she playfully shook her finger at Victor over some remark he made.

Victor didn't spare me a single glance. Not once. It was as if the only girl in the room, as far as he was concerned, was Alexandra Highsmith. Kyle and I finished our lunch, then left.

"The day you come in to go to the library, let me know and I'll meet you," Kyle said. "I've got to get back to work. See you later, Holly."

"Thanks for the lunch." But I wasn't really thinking about food or the next time I'd see Kyle. As I hobbled down the street to the car, I wondered what Zandra had said to Victor to poison him against me.

My uncle's disposition had improved slightly by the time we got back home. He had inventoried his collection thoroughly and, satisfied nothing more had been taken, called the local police to report the missing marionette.

An officer came out to Blackbird Keep, examined the lock on the toy-room door perfunctorily and concurred with Uncle Walker that it was an inside job, which was obvious even to a three-year-old, since the key was under the umbrella stand. Which also shifted the blame back to someone *in* the house—someone who had something to gain or a point to get across. The doll could turn up almost anywhere, the policeman allowed. But they would check antique stores and pawnshops periodically to see if the puppet surfaced.

I expected Uncle Walker to stagger under this disheartening blow, knowing his poor Rapunzel could end up on the wrong side of the tracks in some riffraffy pawnshop where she would undoubtedly pick up bad habits. But he seemed to be his usual professorial self, curious about the progress of my leg, even helping his wife fix dinner later.

All afternoon I tried to shanghai Zandra long enough to ask her about Victor, but the opportunity didn't present itself until after supper. Even then she suddenly made herself indispensible, staying in the kitchen with her mother to wash the dishes, an Alexandra Highsmith first.

She and Aunt Gray joined me and Uncle Walker on the porch to catch the cooling breezes. Walker regaled us with an amusing story during his days at Oxford. Zandra brayed like a donkey, encouraging him to tell more, as if her father had suddenly become the funniest man since Johnny Carson.

I was on to her little tricks. I thought I could outwait her. When she got ready to go to bed, I'd leave with her and nail her about Victor. But the night shadows grew longer and longer and I gave up the ghost before she did.

"'Night, everybody," I said, pulling open the screen door with the last ounce of strength my body possessed. Going to the doctor's and having my cast off must have been more of a strain than I anticipated.

I didn't bother turning on the light in my room. I leaned my crutches against the closet door, shucked off my skirt and top and slipped into my dorm shirt. When I reached down to yank back the covers, my hand touched something . . . not the pillow, but something hard and smooth.

Yanking back my hand as if it had been scalded, I flicked on the light switch, nearly tipping over the lamp.

The jester lay in my bed, his head on my pillow, covers pulled up neatly to his pointed chin. He grinned wickedly at me.

Chapter Ten

I *will not* scream! I ordered myself firmly, though a shriek rattled in the back of my throat. I knew who had done this. And I refused to give her the satisfaction. This was undoubtedly a message from Zandra, warning me to steer clear of Victor Denton. Or else trying to convince me to leave Blackbird Keep.

Even without Zandra's sick little joke, I needed no encouragement. But I couldn't leave until my mother's classes were over in Mississippi. Which meant I still had four more weeks to endure my cousin's whims.

But suppose it wasn't Zandra, a small voice queried inside my head. Of course it's her, I reasoned with myself. Who else hates me as much as she does?

The answer burned in my brain as if by a branding iron.

Seth.

My grandfather. Dead these past five years. Yet his malevolent personality was so ingrained in this house, he might have been standing right beside me, urging me to get out of Blackbird Keep. I didn't belong and never would. I was my father's daughter and he had been banished from the kingdom, dishonorably discharged from the Highsmith family.

Stop it! Seth did not do this. He's dead. You feel his spirit because you were ready to receive his signals—without a willing recipient he has no way of communicating. Outside these walls he has no power. He is an empty spirit, trapped in his own keep. And an empty spirit cannot carry a doll upstairs and put it in your bed. Only human hands can do that. Small, feminine hands that can stroke a black cat and stab an Indiana cousin in the back.

Rationalizing made me feel better, in control again. Much as I wanted to march downstairs, jester in hand, and confront Zandra, letting her know such tactics wouldn't faze me, my sensible self decided to return the jester without a word.

Muffling the golden bells that dangled from the doll's cap, I slipped the Maxfield Parrish doll back into the elephant-leg umbrella stand without anyone being the wiser. And when I went to bed, I dreamed I was standing on a pebbled beach like the one in the Rackham print in the hall downstairs. Only I was the long-haired girl with my sister and brothers, who were playing happily in the surf.

In my dream I felt my chest constrict with fear. Someone— or something—was coming toward me down the beach. I didn't want to face it. When I looked down suddenly, the children were gone, snatched like helpless marionettes and imprisoned by...whom? My grandfather? The wind tugged at my hair and wailed inside my head like the sound of lost children crying. I was all alone with no one to protect me.

I awoke with the crying echoing in my ears. I was whimpering into my pillow, still caught up in the reality of the nightmare. As the sun tore through the early-morning haze, turning the sky that peculiar white color that signified another scorching July day, I felt time was running out. If I was going to redeem my father's good name, I had to get going. He would be reinstated as a Highsmith...if I could crack the last barriers before I cracked first.

Uncle Walker announced at breakfast that he was driving into Draper's Heights, ostensibly to get a haircut but more likely to check on the progress of locating his precious Rapunzel. I asked if I could ride along, to go to the library. Zandra piped up that she had some summer reading to catch up on, but for once Aunt Gray overrode her daughter's wishes with an order to clean up her filthy room that brooked no argument. Was Aunt Gray finally learning how to handle her daughter?

I was glad. I didn't want Zandra horning in on my investigation anymore, especially after what she did last night.

"What was my father like when he was a little boy?" I asked my uncle when we were whizzing along the state road. "What did he like to do? Did he have any hobbies or anything?"

Uncle Walker considered my questions a moment, then replied, his tone reflective, "Arthur was the sunny one in the family. I was almost ten when he was born, so I think I was old enough to appreciate a new baby, unlike Mert, who was at the age where he resented Arthur."

"Uncle Mert didn't like my father?" So their animosity went back long before they both fell in love with Kathryn, when they were little kids. As it turned out, this theory was incorrect.

"Only at first," Walker qualified. "Mert outgrew his jealousy when Arthur was old enough to tag along behind him—you know, the adoring younger brother. They were only two years apart and very close. You didn't see Mert without Art and vice versa. They were both scamps, into everything. Mother thought the sun rose on them, though Arthur was her favorite."

Pleased that *someone* apparently cared for my father, I asked, "Why do you think Grandmother liked my father best? Because he was the youngest?"

"Probably," my uncle agreed. The way he spoke told me he harbored no ill feelings against either of his brothers, even though he was the least favored by his mother. That must have hurt. "When Mert and Art were in their teens, I was away at college. Not Oxford—that came later. I attended Bucknell first. I noticed the change in Art when I came home on weekends."

"What kind of a change?" I pressed.

"I'm not sure. Mother died when I was in my freshman year at Bucknell. Father couldn't get over it. He seemed to blame the boys for some reason, claiming they wore her out with all their carrying on." He gave me a sidelong glance. "Mert and Art weren't bad boys, you have to understand. They were just—

high-spirited. A lot of boys are. I guess my parents were too used to having me around. I was quiet, studious. Never made any trouble. My younger brothers burst into that gloomy old house like a breath of fresh air. The way you did, Holly, when you came last month.''

I didn't know what to say. I'd been plotting my escape and counting the days from the minute I crossed the threshold, believing with every fiber that I was unwanted. Then I realized this was an apology of sorts from my uncle, for coming down on me so hard when the marionette disappeared. Could it be I was no longer Public Enemy Number One?

I patted his arm to let him know it was okay, then said, as tactfully as I could, ''I think Zandra feels that way. Kind of like you did, when you were growing up. She keeps to herself, too, and she's basically quiet. Don't you think you and Aunt Gray are—well, too used to having her around, and that's why you don't pay that much attention to her? Though Aunt Gray seems to be changing. She made Zandra stay home to clean her room. When I first came, nobody made Zandra lift a little finger.''

Uncle Walker looked at me again. ''I said this once before, but it bears repeating. You are a very perceptive young lady. I think we all underestimate you, Holly.'' To himself he added, ''The sins of the fathers.'' He shook his head musingly.

''What? What's that about fathers?''

''It's an expression,'' he said. ''The sins of the fathers are visited upon their children. What I meant by that was I'm just as guilty as my father was. He virtually ignored me—then I had a daughter and am doing the very same thing to her. I see that now, thanks to you. And I'll make an effort to rectify matters, if it's not too late.''

''I don't think it is,'' I reassured him.

I didn't know why I made that pitch for my cousin, who was the last person on earth I should have been defending. But what Uncle Walker had said about his childhood pointed out a pattern—the same thing did seem to be happening to Zandra, only she didn't have any younger brothers to act as a buffer between her and her parents. No wonder she was a loner, preferring Alaric and Bob Dylan to the real world.

Since I arrived at Blackbird Keep, impressions from everyone—dead or alive—funneled through me. My father. Zandra. Seth. I found myself viewing their lives through their eyes, sensing their frustrations, experiencing their pain and loneliness. It was beginning to tire me, playing the role of receiver. Yet I had to keep the channel open if I ever wanted to get to the truth between my father and Seth.

In the Mary Riley Stiles Memorial Library, I was given an unasked-for crash course in the Dewey decimal system. The librarian, a prim-lipped lady who looked as if she hadn't seen another living soul in the past forty years, spent fifteen minutes explaining the cataloging system. At last I managed to tell her what I wanted. Books on the works of Fabergé, I was huffily informed, were located in the art section, under the subdivision of jewelry. I found a big, oversize volume on Carl Fabergé and took it to a reading nook away from the baleful glare of the librarian, still obviously miffed I had cut her speech short.

Victor Denton was right. I could never have imagined the splendor of the famous jeweled Easter eggs he mentioned if I hadn't seen pictures. I leafed through the color plates, dazzled by the photographs, before reading any of the accompanying narrative.

There was a lime-green enameled egg, latticed with gold, that opened to reveal a tiny golden coach complete with rock-crystal windows, platinum tires and diamond-and-gold-trellised doors. This was called the Coronation Egg, Nicholas II's gift to his wife, Alexandra, in 1897.

Another egg was a pink enameled fantasy covered with lilies of the valley fashioned from diamonds and pearls. Three jeweled miniature portraits sprang from the top when a hidden catch was pressed. And the orange-tree egg Victor spoke of, set with fabulous gems and mounted on a jade base, secreted a tiny bird that actually warbled.

The text was printed in dense type, but I gulped down the story of Fabergé's life as if it were the latest dirt on my favorite rock star.

Peter Carl Fabergé was the son of Gustav Fabergé, a jeweler and goldsmith who turned the St. Petersburg business over to his son in 1870, when Carl was twenty-four. Fabergé designed the first Imperial Easter egg for Czar Alexander III to give to his wife, Marie Feodorovna—the white egg with the golden chicken. A tradition began. Each egg had to be more fantastic than the one before, always with a surprise inside. When Nicholas II came to the throne in 1896, he presented two eggs each Easter, one to his mother and one to his wife, Alexandra. As far as anyone could reckon, a total of fifty-three Imperial eggs were presented to the two czarinas. Collectors owned some and some remained in the Kremlin. The whereabouts of at least ten were unaccounted for.

A characteristic of Fabergé's work was his enameling technique—the smooth, even quality and texture arrived at by heating the enamels to tremendously high temperatures, a costly and complex process that seemed to be another casualty of the Russian Revolution, for the art was lost.

When the Bolsheviks were at his door in 1918, a poised Fabergé told them calmly to give him time to put on his hat and coat. He later escaped disguised as a courier and died two years later at Lausanne, Switzerland.

Switzerland. Of course. It fit. Seth met a Russian gentleman in Switzerland. Fabergé's companion, perhaps? I read on eagerly.

Fabergé's work, what wasn't seized by the Bolsheviks, was scattered to the four winds of Europe, smuggled out by the fleeing Imperialists. Besides the Easter eggs, there were ikons, vases, clocks, chalices, cigarette cases, picture frames and figurines. Little jewelry made up the Fabergé collection, because the goldsmith was more interested in creating art objects, but there were a number of brooches, pendants and tie pins designed in the style known as art nouveau.

I closed the book softly, reluctant to come back to dreary old Draper's Heights after having visited the court of Nicholas and Alexandra in Imperialist Russia. Life at the turn-of-the-century must have been grand, indeed. Staying at Blackbird Keep had given me more than a taste of those days. The furniture I sat on, the bed I slept in, the quilt I slept under—all things crafted by long-ago hands. No wonder Seth gleefully wrote to Isabelle of yet another surprise he was sending her from Europe. Besides delighting his wife, he knew those things had lasting value—in an age when washing machines and refrigerators were the rage—and felt compelled to preserve the past before it disappeared altogether.

I wondered if perhaps one of those lost Easter eggs was hidden in the house somewhere. If I found it, I could probably sell it for enough money to pay off the mortgage on our house, go to college and have enough left over to take my mother on a trip around the world. I sighed. That was the wishful thinking of a little kid. Practicality told me my grandfather was not lucky or shrewd enough to have one of the fabled eggs fall into his hands.

But the brooch, a simple piece of jewelry, was another matter. The book made it sound as if Fabergé's stuff could be anywhere. Why not here?

"What did I tell you?" a voice said behind me. "I'm glad you didn't take my word for it."

I jumped, dropping the heavy book on the floor, which caused the librarian to pinch her buttonhole-stitched mouth even tighter. "Victor, for heaven's sake! You scared me half to death. What are you doing sneaking up on me like that?"

He grinned, picking up the book. "You're supposed to be quiet in a library. Next time I'll announce my presence with a brass band."

"How did you know I was here?"

"I ran into Walker at the barber shop. He told me you were looking something up in the library. I had a little free time, so I thought I'd say hi."

"You didn't say hi yesterday." I hadn't forgotten the way he practically cut me dead in the coffee shop.

He leaned negligently against a bookcase. "You weren't alone. I figured your boyfriend wouldn't appreciate me coming up and giving you a big kiss."

"Who said anything about a big kiss? 'Hello, Holly' would have sufficed. And Kyle isn't my 'boyfriend.'"

"Zandra said you two were pretty tight."

I wasn't surprised. But I had neither the energy nor the inclination, since the librarian was glaring at us, to explain my relationship with Kyle Thompkins. Dropping my voice, I changed the subject. "What did you mean when you said you're glad I didn't take your word for it? Your word for what?"

He tapped the glossy cover of the Fabergé book. "His works. They are too fabulous to describe. You have to see them—if not in person, then pictures like these. But it's better in person. I saw this—'' He pointed to the lilies of the valley egg depicted on the jacket. "You can't believe how wonderful it is. All those diamonds . . . and the crown of diamonds on top of the miniatures. You don't realize you're even looking at all those rare stones, they're worked into the design so well. What I wouldn't give to own one.''

"You must be crazy," I declared. "I read in here that if somebody sold an Easter egg, they could get a million dollars for it. Where would you get that kind of money?''

He smiled lazily, bringing out his dimples. "I can dream, can't I?''

"Can't we all?" I regarded Victor for a few seconds. Above the charming grin, his eyes were inscrutable, black as the wing feather of Jinx's I'd found in the yard.

"How are you coming with the Great Mystery?" he wanted to know. "Found out any more about your grandfather and the man he met in Switzerland?''

"No. I haven't had time. There was a little excitement after you left the other day . . .'' I decided not to elaborate on the stolen puppet. If Walker hadn't told Victor about it, then it wasn't up to me to spill the beans. "And I had my cast taken off yesterday. It feels so good to get rid of that weight.''

Victor peered under the table and whistled approvingly at my legs, both shaved but one still pallid, as revealed by the denim miniskirt I'd chosen to wear today. The librarian shot him a murderous glance. "I noticed your castless limb in the coffee shop," he said, "but again, it would have been in poor taste to comment on your legs in front of—uh, your friend.''

"I'd better go," I said hastily. "Uncle Walker is probably finished at the barber's by now.''

I put the book on the cart at the end of the aisle with the other books to be shelved. Victor strolled out with me, but turned to head up the street toward the newspaper office, saying he had to get back to work.

Victor Denton was a puzzle. I still didn't know how to take him. I had the feeling he wasn't truly interested in either Zandra or me, but was dallying with us both until he got whatever it was he was really after. Did he suspect Seth might have found a Fabergé Easter egg? Was that what he wanted? But this Fabergé business hadn't come up until a few days ago, when Zandra blabbed in the Ice-House Café that I was on Mission Impossible. If Victor hadn't suggested going over Seth's business letters, we would never have linked the Russian goldsmith to the missing brooch. And Victor had been hanging around Blackbird Keep like a bee around a honeycomb weeks before he learned of my quest.

My head began to throb. Too many loose ends, too many unrelated elements. The brooch. Fabergé. The man Seth met in Switzerland. Jeweled Easter eggs. The Russian Revolution. Jesters and puppets and trained crows and a shattered love affair. It was enough to drive anybody crazy.

Uncle Walker hadn't returned to the car yet, so I sat down on the low stone wall that bordered the granite library steps to wait. I considered going to see Kyle at the garage, but I didn't want to press my luck. I was there only yesterday—if I went over again today, he'd think I was running after him. Even though he had asked me to meet him when I came into town to work in the library, I felt the invitation was more automatic than sincere. No, let Kyle Thompkins come to me for once.

I stretched my legs out in the sun, willing the puny left one to hurry up and catch up with my tanned right leg. A shadow fell across them. I looked up to see Kyle's Aunt Kathryn, wearing a full-skirted sundress and a wide-brimmed picture hat with trailing satin ribbons.

"Artie told me once I had legs like a show girl," she said without preamble. She hitched her skirt up to her knees, posing like Marilyn Monroe, and laughed. "I think he exaggerated! But you could be a dancer."

I patted the sun-warmed stone. "Hello, Kate," I said, remembering she had given me permission to call her that. "Won't you sit down?"

"Thank you, dear." Kathryn sat down next to me in a pouf of full skirts and crinolines. She carried a little plastic pocketbook decorated with flamingos. "I see you have your cast off. Is your leg better?"

"I still have to use crutches for a while until it heals completely." I couldn't believe we were actually having a normal conversation. Kathryn seemed fine today, nothing at all like that broken woman who swore my father loved her, no matter who he wound up marrying.

Under the brim of her cartwheel hat, Kathryn's indigo eyes appraised me. She looked vaguely confused, as if she'd been introduced to me at a cocktail party once years ago but couldn't remember my name and was too embarrassed to admit it.

"It's Holly," I reminded her gently. "Artie's daughter." Apparently reality flashed in and out of Kathryn's mind like the tantalizing glimpse of gold in a miner's pan—there, then quickly gone.

"Oh, yes. Of course." She crossed her hands neatly in her lap. Despite the sweltering heat, she wore short white gloves, like a graduate from one of those stuffy old-fashioned secretarial schools Mom told me about, where the girls were required to wear hats and gloves and have the seams of their stockings straight. Kathryn was definitely stuck in the fifties, but somehow it suited her. If she were suddenly thrust into the present, she'd be more confused than ever.

"I didn't take it, you know," she said suddenly. Her voice was pitched low and there was no trace of the hysteria I heard at that terrible visit to her house.

"I know. Who did, do you think?" I matched her tone, keeping my own voice level, as if we were discussing the high price of strawberries in the grocery store.

"He never liked me. I guess he thought I wasn't good enough for his boys."

It took me a second or two to change gears with her. Now she was talking about my grandfather. "Did he ever tell you that?"

She shook her head and the ribbons on her hat trembled like the leaves of an old calendar fluttering in the breeze. "Not in so many words. But I knew. He hated the sight of me. And once I heard him tell Mert I didn't have the brains of a flea and what did he ever see in me? Seth knew I was listening, too." Tears blurred her lovely blue eyes, like rain washing down a window that looked out over the ocean. She swallowed, visibly regaining composure, and gave a little laugh. "I told Artie what his father said about me. You know what he said? He said it was a case of the pot calling the kettle black. If his brother and father thought I was dumb, then that just showed how dumb *they* were."

My grandfather wasn't dumb by a long chalk, but he did have a vicious streak. Imagine making cruel remarks to a girl as sensitive as Kathryn. "That's right," I agreed. "They were both real stupid. Anybody can see how wonderful you are."

Kathryn smiled tremulously through her tears. I forgot she was older than my mother. At that moment she seemed more my age—she could have been one of my friends at school and I was commiserating over a guy who didn't know she was alive or a rebuff by some callous upperclassman.

"Holly!" It was my uncle, pulling the Daimler up to the curb. "Ready to go?"

Then he saw Kathryn for the first time. His astonishment was evident. She scooped back the deep brim of her hat and stared back at him, her tragic eyes beautiful in full sunlight, years of hurt and bewilderment shining from them. My uncle turned away first, a typical Highsmith, stubborn and unyielding.

I was angry with him when I got into the car. "Why didn't you say hello to her at least?"

He ignored my question. "I didn't know you knew her."

"Does anybody really know that woman?" One person did. My father. And he left her.

Jinx had been trying for days to get into the house. He flew to my shoulder from the lilac bush whenever he saw me, hoping to cadge a ride. He even burrowed under my hair so Uncle Walker wouldn't catch him. He never gave up, and it was comical to witness his determination.

One night I called to him from my bedroom window, which I had opened. He flew in, chuckling to himself at this clever ruse, but he couldn't keep quiet. He screeched radio commercials, until Aunt Gray came into my room and suggested I let the bird out the same window.

I felt sorry for the poor crow, who had once enjoyed the good life and hated to give it up. Could anybody blame him for preferring hamburger at the dinner table to nasty old rabbits or squirrels mashed on the highway?

When we returned from town that day, Uncle Walker went indoors to work on his book, but I stayed outside with Jinx, admiring his pop-top collection and making up silly games, like hiding M&Ms in my pocket or my hair or my ear and letting him find them. He was such a funny bird, and so smart he made the rest of us look like fools. No wonder my grandfather loved training crows.

The late-afternoon sun was sketching long shadows across the yard when I decided it was time to go in. "I have to go now, Jinx," I called to the bird. "Bye!" I braced myself for claws in my shoulder, since he attempted to hitchhike in with me at least once a day.

But no cawing whirlwind landed on my shoulder. He had been here a minute ago—where had he gone? I hobbled around to the side of the house just in time to see black tail feathers disappear into the ivy that covered the stone chimney and the entire wall.

Jinx had managed to sneak into the house after all. Through the window of the toy room. It wasn't possible. I knew my uncle never opened those windows, and in any case, the ivy clung to that side of the house like barnacles. Yet Jinx was in the toy room—I was certain.

I tugged at a tendril of ivy trailing to the ground. It wasn't fastened at all, but hung over the brickwork like a curtain. Under the ivy veil, the ancient vines had been pruned into a ladder of sorts, leading up to the windows of the toy room. From here I could see that one of the diamond-shaped panes was missing. That was how Jinx got into the house.

And who else? Who had made this ladder and why?

I hung onto the vine with one hand, pondering my discovery. Jinx was bright but he wasn't that bright. He couldn't have knocked out a windowpane or hacked the ivy into a ladder. His capabilities were limited to copying. He must have watched someone climb the ivy, then poke out the pane. Being a bird, he didn't need the ivy ladder—he simply flew up to the window and squeezed himself through the broken pane.

There were two smart cookies around here. Jinx...and who else?

In the undergrowth behind me I heard the unmistakable crunch of footsteps. Before I could turn around to see who it was, something blunt and heavy struck me on the back of my head.

The gnarled vine raked my palm as I slid to the ground.

Chapter Eleven

I always imagined heaven would be peaceful, a beautiful garden with a host of angels singing in the background and cloud-soft couches to loll around on.

If I had died and gone to heaven, then I was in for a rude shock. Whatever I was lying on was lumpy and uncomfortable and my choir of angels sounded like the harsh cries of crows.

It was a crow. Jinx was driving someone away with his strident *caw-caw-caw!*

I rolled over and sat up. I was definitely not in heaven, unless all the heavenly gardeners had elected to go on strike. My head hurt and a wicked scratch in the middle of my palm dripped blood. The sight of bright-red blood rolling off my hand into the dusty weeds brought me back to the present.

Someone had hit me. And Jinx, ever the protector, was heckling my attacker right this very instant. I struggled to my feet, fumbling for my crutches. I could hear Jinx's screams down past the aviary and knew they were heading for the deep woods behind the estate. Even if I could run, I'd never catch him now.

I rubbed the lump on the back of my head gingerly, trying to remember if I had seen anything before blacking out. There was a half instant in which I'd sensed someone was in the bushes behind me, and then I turned...and was clobbered. But didn't I catch a glimmer of white out of the corner of my eye before darkness descended? Like the white of a gown, or a woman's dress.

Moments later, Jinx flew toward me, wings beating with the effort of pursuit. He cawed excitedly from the willow tree until I was able to coax him onto my shoulder.

"Who was it?" I asked him, while he poked his beak unsuccessfully into my ear and under my collar, looking for stray M&Ms. "Who hit me?"

Of course he couldn't answer. He was only a crow, after all, not a stool pigeon. I marveled that he left the toy room to defend my honor, even if he couldn't tell me who conked me on the noggin.

I wasn't really hurt, aside from a sore spot on my head. In fact, I wasn't even frightened by the incident. I felt convinced that someone was more interested in scaring me off than trying to harm me.

"You're a good bird," I praised him. "A king among crows." He had sacrificed hard-won entry into the house to come back outside and rescue me.

His Highness responded by pulling my hair. "Coke is it!" he shrieked most unroyally.

"Is that so?" I had to laugh despite everything. "If Madison Avenue ever got hold of you, they'd make a fortune!"

Aunt Gray came around the corner then. "Holly, haven't you heard me calling you in to dinner?"

"Sorry, Aunt Gray. I've been—sort of busy with Jinx. Teaching him a new trick," I improvised.

"He knows plenty of tricks as it is. What was that racket he was making a few minutes ago? I could swear he was after somebody."

"That was part of the trick," I said smoothly. "Where's Zandra? I haven't seen her all afternoon."

Aunt Gray led the way back to the house. "In her room still. She's been cleaning since ten this morning. It was such a wreck I wouldn't be surprised if it took her the rest of the week."

But Zandra wasn't in her room. She was pouring iced tea into glasses. She handled the pitcher calmly enough, but I noticed

beads of perspiration on her upper lip. Her white T-shirt and
shorts were dirty, but then she had been cleaning her room all
day. Or had she? Was she sweating from the sweltering
heat...or from a dash through the woods? She could have
bumped me on the head, then run into the woods behind the
aviary, doubling back when Jinx gave up the fight. It was en-
tirely possible that she sneaked up the stairs without Aunt Gray
seeing her, washed up in the bathroom and then came back
down again when Aunt Gray went outside to look for me.

If she was my attacker, she hid it well, taking her place across
from me at the table, passing the butter and sugar bowl non-
chalantly as if we were tablemates at a banquet benefiting
Children's Hospital or something.

It was almost too hot to eat. The four of us picked at the
pasta salad and croissants Aunt Gray had fixed. A platter of
fresh vegetables purchased from the roadside market outside of
town held tempting slices of tomatoes, cucumbers and icicle-
white scallions. I nibbled an onion and ate half a croissant,
apologizing to Aunt Gray that the heat had robbed my appetite.

"Perhaps some ice cream later," she said, understanding.
This evening even she looked wilted in a limp cotton sundress.
Uncle Walker drank two glasses of tea, one right after the other,
eating less than I did. Only Zandra finished her helping of salad
and bread. Could someone who had hit her cousin not an hour
before eat pasta salad so blithely if she wasn't innocent? Maybe
I was wrong about her.

If the attacker doesn't come back and kill me, I thought as I
went upstairs to my room, the humidity will. Not one breath of
air circulated in my room. The blue-and-yellow calico curtains
at the windows hung down as if lead weights had been sewn into
the hems.

Zandra came to the door lugging a floor fan. "Uncle Walker
thought you ought to have this," she said, setting the fan next
to the dresser. Her cat, Alaric, footpadded in behind her like a
black shadow.

"This didn't come from their room, did it?" I asked. "I
don't want anyone else to roast just because I'm a guest."

She shook her head. "Mom and Dad have a window fan and I have one just like this. We usually keep this fan downstairs, but it's so hot tonight you won't sleep a wink without it."

As if I could relax enough to shut my eyes, suspecting my cousin in the very next room of assault and battery. "Thanks," I said, and that was all. She'd barely spoken two words to me this week; I didn't have to kiss her feet in undying gratitude simply because she brought me a fan.

She hesitated in the doorway, indicating she wanted to stay and talk, but I busied myself plugging in my fan and adjusting the control knob. What did we have to say to each other at this point? In a few weeks I would leave and never have to think about Alexandra Highsmith again. This summer was a chapter in my life I wanted to forget. She left, and with a disdainful flick of his tail, her cat followed.

The fan directed a blast of hot air toward my bed, but it was better than nothing. I crawled to the bottom of my bed, closer to the windows and the last light of the day, propped my pillow on the footboard and began reading Seth's account of his studies with blackbirds.

The journal was tough going until I reached the part where my grandfather found a hatchling. In the woods bordering Blackbird Keep some men had cut down a tree. Seth heard the distress cries of birds and found a nest in the treetop. Two of the babies were dead, but the third peeped hopefully when Seth parted the leafy branches. He took the orphan home, and his life-long love affair with crows began.

Edgar Allan Poe, according to my grandfather, was the cleverest bird that ever drew breath. He taught Poe to count by marking empty oatmeal boxes with dots, then hiding a piece of fish cake inside one. The bird learned to count up to six. Seth also recorded the calls of the wild crows around Blackbird Keep. There were many different kinds of calls—an assembly call to drive off an enemy or get help; a slow, stretched-out all-clear call; a fast, frantic danger signal. Seth calculated that the different combinations of caws rarely exceeded six—very occasionally they extended to nine. He believed Poe's ability to count to six had to do with the limited "sentence structure" of crows.

From a biologist at the university Seth learned that crows have special muscles on either side of their trachea that enable them to mimic. Because of their highly developed brains—for birds—crows adapt quickly to changing circumstances. Even when heavily persecuted by man, their greatest enemy, the crow population actually increases. "When there is nothing left on earth," this scientist concluded wryly, "there will still be crows."

The rest of Seth's notes detailed the antics of Edgar Allan Poe, mischief maker *extraordinaire*. Some of the things Seth wrote about Poe made Jinx seem as docile as a canary. Like the time my grandmother baked a birthday cake for one of the boys. Poe sat on the counter and watched the fascinating operation of my grandmother slathering frosting on with a small knife and then placing dime-store candles around the crown of the cake. When she turned her back, he plucked out the candles, then grabbed the knife in his beak and carefully scraped off the icing, throwing globs of it all over the counter, which he then tracked around the kitchen, making an even bigger mess.

Poe fell in love once with a wild crow Seth called Annabel Lee. Seth gave the happy couple his blessing, delighted when they built a nest in the chimney because he could observe family behavior firsthand. But before a single egg was laid, Poe and his lady love had a tiff and she flew the coop. The nest stayed, becoming more weather-ragged as the years ticked by. Seth never explained why he left it there. A tribute to lost love?

Poe was succeeded by other birds: two grackles named Nostradamus and Merlin, a one-legged blue jay named Jake, and three less-distinguished crows called Crony, Crocus and Crochet. The last three names seemed out of place until I pronounced them aloud. I had to admire my grandfather's sense of humor, at least in naming his birds.

And then of course there was a whole section devoted to his last crow, aptly christened Jinx. At this stage in his life Seth was apparently slowing down. He let Jinx have the run of the house, which made him a very spoiled bird. No wonder Walker and Gray found him insufferable. Seth spent a good share of his last years in his room, watching TV or listening to the radio and feeding Jinx tidbits from the trays Aunt Gray brought into him. This was where Jinx picked up his repertoire of commercials.

Even now, on the rare occasions he was allowed to stay indoors on his T-shaped perch, he was rapt before the television set, making contented cooing sounds and lifting his feathers, which Seth believed also showed pleasure. I wondered if the bird somehow associated the talking box with his lord and master.

Poor Jinx. The man who raised him was gone, leaving him behind in the dubious care of an indifferent family.

I sat up, letting the book drop to my lap. Suppose I took Jinx home with me? Uncle Walker and Aunt Gray would be thrilled to get rid of him. I could probably locate an old cage in the shed out back so he could fly back to Miller's Forks with me. But then I realized the reception we'd get from my mother would be less than welcoming. I could hear her now: "A bird in the house, Holly? Are you out of your mind? Don't we have enough to do around here with Pipkin?"

Sighing, I picked up the book, intending to put it on the nightstand. As I did, a packet of photographs and papers fell on the quilt. A pocket like those used in library books had been pasted to the back cover, and the papers had been tucked inside.

With nervous fingers I separated the pictures and envelopes into two piles. There were letters in the envelopes—the missing correspondence between Seth and Isabelle during the year 1934. I scanned them eagerly, searching for any reference to the brooch or Seth's mysterious dinner with the Russian he'd met in Switzerland.

These letters were different in tone from the others—not so loving. In fact, Seth and Isabelle carried on a quarrel. Isabelle wanted her husband to come home; Seth insisted he couldn't leave his business. Things looked pretty rocky, and I sensed their marriage was threatened. In the last letter Seth appeased his unhappy wife with the promise of a present, without a hint of what it was. He closed the letter with an odd request: "And if we ever have a daughter I'd like her to be named Alexandra."

That was it. I turned to the photographs, knowing they were the pictures from the album. Why had my grandfather hidden the letters and snapshots in this book? Maybe he couldn't deal with unsettling painful events so he put any reminders of them out of sight.

I stared at the photos, incredulous. Baby pictures, pictures of toddlers, pictures of young boys in Sunday-best suits, school pictures.

I bounded across the room to retrieve the photo album from the dresser drawer where I stored it, unwilling to give it back to Aunt Gray since it seemed to be the only link to my father, even if his pictures were gone. Flipping heedlessly through the photographs of my grandparents, I located the blank pages with the white-inked captions indicating snapshots of Merton and then Arthur. The first two pictures fitted within the hinged rectangles exactly. My grandmother had even repeated the captions on the backs of the photographs so there could be no mix-up if the pictures were taken out.

Quickly I slipped pictures into their matching niches until the album was complete once again, scarcely believing I had photographs of my father in my possession at last.

He was just as Walker had described, a sunny baby grinning into the camera, a sturdy toddler with one leg hooked over the rail of his playpen—even then anxious to leave—an impish first-grader minus two front teeth.

In one photograph my father was holding one of the crows on an outstretched arm—"Arthur and Friend, July 1952," was all my grandmother had written below. He appeared to be eight or nine, with long skinny legs sticking out beneath baggy shorts, Band-Aids crisscrossing one knee. The picture was taken outdoors—I recognized the willow tree in the side yard—but what struck me the most was my father's posture. He leaned a little to one side, as if bracing himself against a big wind.

At home in the box in my mother's closet was a picture of me around that age, standing exactly the same way, "leaning toward Funston," which Mom claimed Daddy used to say. My throat tightened. Like father like daughter. He'd given me another trait besides tea-colored eyes; the way I stand. There was more to it than the fact my spine curved to make me stand that way. It was an attitude toward life we shared. We might bow under adversity, but we would never fall.

I slipped this picture from the album and put it in my purse. No one had missed it all these years, and I really wanted to have it.

There were snapshots of my father with his brothers, most particularly Merton. Merton didn't look like either his father or mother, whereas both Walker and Arthur clearly resembled Seth. Merton's mouth had a sullen set to it and his eyes were darker than his brothers'. Because the pictures were all black and white, I couldn't determine if Mert's eyes were dark brown...or a very dark indigo. Though I scrutinized every picture Merton appeared in, it was really impossible to tell.

The next day was grocery day again. I was up bright and early, helping Aunt Gray with breakfast and her grocery list so we could be on our way.

In the car Zandra and her mother made plans to go shopping for school clothes. I sat in the backseat, listening to the first real conversation I'd heard exchanged between them. Zandra seemed genuinely interested in her mother's advice on what styles to purchase, and when I suggested they stop in the drugstore and buy a bunch of the latest fashion magazines, they both agreed this was the ideal solution.

"I'm going to throw away anything over a year old," my cousin decreed. "I'll just toss stuff in a box for the Salvation Army so I'll have room for new things."

I almost wished I could be around when the Salvation Army made their first refusal ever in history. Yet I felt a small stab of jealousy. Buying a whole new wardrobe was something I'd never get to experience, not with the money crunch at our house.

"Coming with us, Holly?" Aunt Gray asked when we arrived at the Safeway.

"Would you mind if I didn't?"

Zandra gave me a feline grin. "Holly's got bigger fish to fry. I'll bet you're going to see Kyle Thompkins, aren't you?"

As a matter of fact I was, but before I could make a snappy retort Aunt Gray said, "Since you'll be going that way, why don't you stop by the newspaper office and ask Victor if he'd like to come to dinner tonight? We haven't seen him in a while. Maybe he feels uncomfortable without an invitation."

"He didn't used to," I couldn't resist saying. "He used to drop in unannounced all the time."

I thought Zandra's face would light up at the prospect of dining with the suave and charming Mr. Denton. Instead she remarked flatly, "We'd better beat the crowds, Mom." Hardly the reaction you'd expect from a girl who swooned whenever Victor's name was mentioned. Perhaps the bloom was off the rose.

Kyle was disemboweling a tottery-looking Pinto when I arrived at the garage. He set down the crankcase or whatever he was holding when he saw me and wiped his hands on a towel looped through the door handle of the car.

"Hi, Holly," he said, coming toward me.

"Hi. Think it'll live?"

"Oh, sure. I patch 'em up and send them on their merry way again until something else breaks down." He saw my expression and killed the banter. "What's up?"

"Plenty. Yesterday I found a ladder in the ivy outside my uncle's toy room. Someone had also knocked out a pane of glass in the window. That's how the burglar got in the house and stole the puppet. And what's more, whoever did it hit me on the head. But it was too late. I'd already found the ladder."

"Whoa!" He put up a hand to halt me. "What on earth are you babbling about? Somebody climbed an ivy ladder and stole a puppet?"

"Oh, that's right. I didn't tell you about the break-in."

"No, you didn't. What other secrets are you keeping?" He eyed me suspiciously.

"The last time I saw you we talked about the brooch. I forgot about Rapunzel."

Now he looked thoroughly baffled. " 'Rapunzel'?"

Slowly, so he wouldn't think I was crazier than I already was, I related the incident of the break-in, winding up with my discovery of the ivy ladder and the bop on my head.

He leaned against the fender of the car, trying to digest the whole story. "Now let me get this straight. The day Victor goes through Seth's business letters and finds something that could tie into the missing brooch, somebody breaks in your uncle's collection and steals a valuable marionette."

"Go to the head of the class—you got it right the first time."

"And the key is in the hallway the whole time?"

"Under this umbrella stand that looks like an elephant's—"

"Spare me any more gruesome details," he protested. "So whoever took this puppet had to know what they were doing. It wasn't a random thing at all."

"I guess. But they could have taken anything in my uncle's collection—it's all rare and valuable."

"And your uncle is positive he checked the lock before he went in to dinner?" I nodded. Kyle rubbed his forehead. "So whoever broke in really knew his way around the house, wouldn't you say?"

"You think it was Victor," I blurted out. "Just because he comes around a lot."

"Has he been back since the robbery?" Kyle asked.

I considered a second. "No, he hasn't. But he gets busy with his job and we don't see him for several days at a time."

Kyle seemed to accept this. "Who do you think hit you on the head yesterday? Did you see anything at all?"

I didn't want to answer. Yet I had to tell him about the flash of white I thought I saw just before I blanked out.

He caught my drift immediately. "White, like a white dress? Like the dress my Aunt Kathryn wore the night she wandered around the garden?"

"Or like the white shorts Zandra was wearing yesterday," I said. "Whoever hit me didn't hit very hard. You know, like the way a girl—or a woman—would hit somebody. I wasn't out long and my head hardly hurt. It was more of a glancing blow."

"But you don't really think it was your cousin, do you?"

"I don't know. Why would anyone hit me in the first place?"

"Because you found the secret entry into the house. Whoever made that ladder was obviously planning to use it again."

The full import of his words sank in. "And I know about it. Am I in danger?" I asked.

"I doubt it. If what you say is true, a real featherweight beaned you. That hardly sounds like much of a threat." He narrowed his midnight eyes at me. "Besides, Aunt Kathryn wouldn't hurt a flea."

We were back to that again. "Kyle," I said wearily, "I never said I thought it was your aunt. You did. I don't think she did it any more than I think my cousin did. Why would your aunt climb into the house and steal a puppet? It doesn't make sense."

"It doesn't make sense to accuse your cousin, either. She *lives* there."

But he didn't really know Zandra. She was capable of almost anything. As usual, our discussion went around and around in futile circles. Kyle was so defensive about his aunt. Plus he still had trouble remembering I was on his side, even if my last name was Highsmith.

"She could have taken it to get back at Seth," Kyle was saying. "Even though he's dead, she could steal something his son valued to get back at him that way."

"I think we're reaching," I told him. "I want to keep an open mind until I find out more. It's not fair to jump to conclusions and accuse either your aunt or my cousin or Victor Denton. That's what happened years ago—people made false accusations and other people got hurt." I paused, turning a thought over in my mind. "I think Kathryn would like the past buried so she can get on with what's left of her life."

"What makes you say that?"

"I saw her the other day—the day I came to the library to find out about Fabergé. We sat on the wall outside and talked a bit. She told me she didn't take it."

"Take what?"

I stopped, my mouth open. "Well—the brooch, I guess." At least that's what I *assumed* she'd been talking about. Suppose she meant my uncle's marionette? "Of course she meant the brooch," I said hurriedly. "She couldn't have known about the puppet."

But Kyle already heard suspicion in my tone. "That's right. Blame the crazy lady. Blame her for everything. She's a convenient scapegoat. She always has been where your family is concerned."

"Kyle—"

"You're just as bad as the rest of them. Saying one thing, thinking another. Excuse me," he said, his voice like flint. "I have to get back to work."

There was nothing to say. He bent over the engine of the Pinto again, leaving me standing there. I left without looking back.

I wanted to cry, but didn't dare let tears flow on the street. Remembering that Aunt Gray had asked me to invite Victor Denton to dinner that night, I hobbled into the office of the *Sentinel*.

A receptionist sitting in front of a number of glass-walled cubicles told me Victor Denton was out on assignment in the next town.

"Do you know when he'll be back?" I asked.

"Depends. If he gets lost again, it might be pretty late."

I managed a smile. "Victor Denton gets lost? Not the Boy Wonder."

"'Fraid so. He's pretty new around here. You can't expect anybody to learn the ropes in just a few months."

Something fell away inside me. "What do you mean 'few months'? I thought Victor had been working here almost a year."

"Oh, no, honey. I don't know what he's been feeding you, but Victor was hired the end of May—not three months ago."

Chapter Twelve

You guys go ahead. I'll stay here," I told Uncle Walker. He was standing on the porch with Aunt Gray and Zandra, waiting for me.

"You're not going?" he said.

"My leg's bothering me. I think I'd rather stay home." I fibbed. My leg didn't bother me a bit.

"Are you sure, Holly? It's supposed to be a really good movie." To her husband Aunt Gray added, "Maybe we ought to stay here with Holly if she's not feeling well."

"No, no! This is the last night they're showing this movie and I know how much you want to see it. I'll catch it later, when I get home, maybe. Please don't let me spoil your evening. I'll be fine."

"Well . . . if you're sure . . ." Aunt Gray was still dubious.

"Positive. You'd better hurry if you want to get there in time." I waved at them until the Daimler was out of sight. They were gone.

I had two reasons for wanting to stay home. Both were important, but one was vital.

Zandra brought up the movie when I informed Aunt Gray and her I couldn't find Victor to invite him to dinner. I decided not to tell them what the receptionist in the newspaper office had revealed, that he had been in town only a few months, not nearly a year as he'd led us to believe.

"Then let's go see that new Harrison Ford movie playing in Odessa," Zandra suggested. "We won't even bother with dinner. We'll just eat junk at the movie."

Much as Aunt Gray wanted to get along better with her daughter, she wasn't about to lower her standards of civilization. "The movie sounds wonderful, but we'll eat supper at home. Your father expects something more substantial than a bucket of popcorn. I think it's about time we treated Holly. She's hardly been out of the house since she arrived."

I went along with the movie plans until they were ready to leave. I knew how important this evening was to them—the first time they'd gone out as a family in ages. They could iron out their problems and have a good heart-to-heart a lot easier without me around.

That was one reason I bowed out. The second was more selfish. I needed time alone to think. So much had happened lately I hadn't had a chance to sort out any of it. All I could do these days was react, like an inept left fielder who kept ducking the balls instead of catching them. Kyle had laid a pretty heavy trip on me earlier, Victor had lied about his job on the *Sentinel* and someone had tried to prevent me from finding the ladder in the ivy outside the toy room . . . peripheral problems that distracted me from learning what had happened between my father and Seth.

As I was turning to go back inside, it suddenly occurred to me I would never find that out. Both my father and Seth were dead, their differences buried with them. They didn't settle the score between them while they were alive—though I suspected both wanted to, only didn't know how to go about it—and it wasn't likely I could do that for them now.

A weight seemed to lift off my shoulders. Ever since Uncle Walker's letter had come, inviting me to stay at Blackbird Keep for the summer, I had been pulled toward this house. And when

I arrived, I became some sort of mediator between the dead and the living. An unwitting pawn in a game that had begun twenty-five years ago and would never be finished.

Seth's spirit was just that—the remains of a personality too strong to dim. He'd been miserable most of his life. I don't think he was capable of being happy after his wife died, and his sons suffered because of it.

But my father left Blackbird Keep and never looked back. He started a new life with my mother, and though times had been tight, they'd been happy. My memories of him were bright and glowing, lit from an unseen source like the Maxfield Parrish pictures in Uncle Walker's study. I wanted to keep them that way.

Jinx cawed from the lilac bush. He had seen the family drive off and knew I was home alone.

"Want in, do you?" I asked, opening the screen door wide. "I shouldn't do this. You'd better behave in here or else."

He sailed in, his wings ruffling the sultry air in the hallway, and landed on the elephant-leg umbrella stand. Spotting the brass bells bobbling from the jester's satin cap, he reached out and picked at one.

"I told you to behave!" I scolded. "You're not in the house two seconds and already you're causing trouble! No wonder Aunt Gray doesn't want you in here."

But crows are persistent, especially if they see something shiny and tempting. Jinx worried the brass bell until I stomped over to shoo him away, afraid he'd rip it off. Uncle Walker would have classic conniptions if anything happened to his prized jester.

Flapping my crutch at him, I yelled, "Leave it alone, will you? You're just as bad as Poe, always steal—"

I stopped in midflap.

That was it. I couldn't tackle all the unanswered questions floating around this house, but I could solve one puzzle.

I bent to give Jinx a quick peck on his little black head. "Jinx, you're a genius!" I stared at the jester, who grinned back unswervingly as always. It was time I made peace with the Keeper of the Hall. "You knew all along, didn't you?" I asked the doll. "Even though Uncle Walker got you years after it happened, you knew the truth."

Was it silly to attribute human characteristics to a bird and a wooden toy? I didn't think so. In their own ways, Jinx and the jester had absorbed events the people living in this house were too busy to notice. It's the little things that elude our attention.

I wanted to share my revelation with someone. Not someone—Kyle. I could call him, but suppose I was wrong? I had to do this myself. Then I would show him.

"Come outside with me," I told the crow, shooing him back out the door. "We've got work to do."

The summer evening was still and expectant, as if waiting for something to happen. Twilight was slipping around the edges of the late-setting sun, which lay like a crimson fireball on the western horizon. Not a leaf stirred. The weeds and flowers in the backyard drooped from the heat. In the top of the venerable willow, grackles creaked at one another, the weight of their bodies causing the slender branches to bow and sway.

Jinx flew ahead of me as I fought my way down the chickory-choked path to the old shed. The lock on the splintered door was practically fossilized. With my shoulder to the door I slammed my body against it. The hinges screeched in protest, but the door gave. I stepped over the crumbling granite sill and into a tiny musty-smelling room crammed with rakes and grass shears. Suspended on spikes above the single paint-spattered window was exactly what I needed. A ladder.

The ladder wasn't heavy, but I couldn't carry it while on crutches. I leaned them against the toolshed door, knowing I couldn't use them where I was going, anyway.

Before propping the ladder against the stone chimney of the toy-room wing, I stooped to examine the weeds around its base, then lifted the ivy curtain that veiled the footholds pruned in the ancient vines. As far as I could tell, no one had disturbed the site since yesterday. A good sign. Maybe whoever made the ivy ladder had gotten what he—or she—wanted, after all, and had no reason to come back.

Too bad I couldn't use the ladder already there, but with my weak leg, I couldn't take any chances. One slip and I knew my leg would never be strong enough to recover—I would surely fall.

Steadying the ladder against the chimney, I began to climb. The ladder had evidently been hanging in the shed for aeons, because I touched all kinds of dead bugs and abandoned spider webs stuck to the rungs as I crawled upward. Any other time I would have screamed or at least winced, but this was no time to be squeamish. I had a mission to accomplish and I had to do it before my aunt and uncle got back from the movies. If they saw me scaling a ladder to the roof, they'd throw a fit, knowing I'd had my cast removed just days ago and was still under a doctor's care.

When I reached the top rung, the ladder began to wobble, so I grabbed the lip of the eave out-thrust over my head and hung on, trying to figure out the best way to get on the roof. I looked down. The ground wasn't all that far away, because the wing was only one story. But the roof slanted high above me, pitched at a sharp angle. Then I noticed the "snow eagles," ornamental brass cleats studded at intervals along the surface of the roof, which were supposed to keep snow from sliding off. Only old houses had them.

And I was glad. They would come in really handy. The roof was slate and as treacherous as a greased sliding board. Hitching myself up so I could reach over the eave, I clutched a pair of snow eagles and hoisted myself up until I was lying on the roof, my feet braced against the cleats. I inched my way up the roof in this manner until I was straddling the ridge.

"Don't look down," I cautioned myself as I scooted toward the chimney on the end. My goal was a bunch of sticks and twigs stuffed into the mouth of the chimney. Edgar Allan Poe's nest, the one Seth allowed to clutter the chimney after Poe's girlfriend deserted him at the altar.

Jinx thought I was playing a new game. He swooped around the chimney, shrieking, "Where's the beef!" until I yelled at him to light someplace, he was making me nervous.

He settled on my shoulder, naturally. As if I weren't handicapped enough. "Where's the beef!" he screamed again.

"It better be in here," I said, hugging the chimney between both knees so I could have my hands free.

I fished through the crow's nest, which could hardly be called a nest after years of wind and snow and rain had battered it into an unrecognizable mess of sticks. I scooped out fistfuls of leaves, throwing them into the air like confetti from a long-ago party. When my fingers touched something hard and metallic, I held my breath. I pulled out a tarnished baby spoon. With my shirttail I wiped off some of the grime on it. There was a date engraved in the filigreed handle: October 15, 1942. Who did this belong to? My father was born in 1944, I knew. Was this Merton's baby spoon?

Still, it wasn't what I knew had to be in this nest. I poked deeper into the twigs and pulled out an amazing array of items. A fifty-cent piece, a crown-shaped finial from a lamp, two brass door keys, one skate key, a buttonhook, a tin angel from a Christmas tree…and one Fabergé brooch, lost for twenty-five years. Edgar Allan Poe's booty.

I jammed the other junk in my pockets, but I held the brooch in my hand, wondering how such a small piece of jewelry could cause so much trouble to so many people during the past quarter century.

The pin was not what I hoped for. Ever the optimist, I had been praying my grandfather had somehow managed to smuggle one of the ten unaccounted-for Easter eggs into Blackbird Keep. And when my fingers closed around the brooch, I knew there would be no priceless Fabergé egg, but perhaps the pin would be set with rubies and emeralds.

It wasn't. Only seed pearls circled the gold-rimmed oval, while enameled turquoise flowers filled in the center. As ignorant as I was about jewelry, the enameling felt smooth and rich under my fingertips, and even in the dying light I identified the two-headed Imperial eagle on the back, the hallmark of Fabergé.

Had the brooch been missing since that afternoon my father had promised Kathryn he'd give it to her one day? Kathryn said they'd found the pin, but perhaps my father dropped it again, in the long grass where the beady eyes of a too-smart-for-his-own-good crow spied it. Poe carried his prize off to his nest, and that's where it'd been all these years. I guess no one would ever know. My biggest problem now was getting back down.

Or so I thought.

Directly across from my line of vision was the ancient willow. As I stared at it, the last long shafts of light arrowed into the tree, illuminating the topmost branches and creating menacing shadows below. The tree suddenly shifted from innocent to sinister, just like the tree in the Rackham picnic scene over my bed. I remembered my initial observation of Blackbird Keep: nothing was as it seemed.

Too late I realized someone was climbing the ladder.

I shoved the Fabergé pin in my pocket and edged back from the chimney. Where was I going? Whoever it was had control of the ladder, the only exit down.

When Victor Denton's head appeared over the roof, I wasn't surprised. All along I suspected what he was after, but only now did I acknowledge my instincts.

"You can't have it," I told him, angry that I had let myself be taken in by his phony charms.

"Give it here, Holly," he said. His feet were braced on the last rung of the ladder, but he was still brave enough to hold out one hand. The pirate wasn't even sweating. His white shirt and pants looked as fresh as a mint julep. "You'll save us both a lot of grief if you just give it to me."

My Highsmith stubbornness came out in full force. "I will *not* just give it to you. I found it. It belongs to the family. Who are you to tell me to hand it over? You liar. You haven't worked in this town a year. You've only been here a few more weeks than I have."

He sighed. "I can see you're going to make me resort to unscrupulous methods. Let me put it to you this way, Holly. If you don't hand me the brooch, I'm coming up there to get it. And if I have to climb up there, I won't be such a gentleman. I'll get the pin, even if there is only one of us left on this roof."

The implication of his threat chilled my blood. He was going to throw me off the roof! Ordinarily I wouldn't be panic-stricken, since the wing was only one story. If I fell, I probably wouldn't be terribly hurt, just banged up. But my leg! A fall like that would fracture my half-healed leg again. I could be lame for life!

"Are you going to hand the pin over nicely?" Victor asked, his dimpled grin adding insult to injury. He knew I knew what would happen if he pitched me off the roof. "I'm going to count to five...one—"

I cast my glance around the roof, desperately searching for another way out. If only there were a skylight or—

"Two..." His eyes were as black as the tarnish on the baby spoon I'd found in Poe's nest.

I tried reasoning with him. "Wait! Why do you want the pin so bad, anyway? You haven't even seen it. It's not that great, only a few seed pearls—"

"Three..."

"You hit me on the head, didn't you?" I hedged. Of course—the white pants and shirt. "You were the one who cut the ivy, weren't you?" Perspiration was running down the backs of my knees, making the slate roofing even more slippery.

"Four...five." His hands reached over the eave. He was coming to get me.

Action exploded around us as several things happened at once.

From out of nowhere, Jinx dived and pecked Victor on the head, wheeling in midair to attack again.

"What the—" Victor threw his arms over his head.

Then a voice called up, "Merton Highsmith! Come down here this instant! You leave Holly alone!"

While Jinx was zeroing in on Victor's head again, I leaned over to see who the newcomer was. Kathryn stood at the base of the ladder, wearing a filmy white dress, her dark-blue eyes blazing.

"Do you hear me, Mert? I said come down and leave her alone!"

"Jinx, stop!" I commanded. "Enough!" When the bird backed off to perch in the willow, I stared at Victor. "You can't be Merton Highsmith. You're too young."

But not too young to be his son, I realized. I had seen those unfathomable black eyes before, in the photo album. Merton, the brother in the middle, the one who didn't inherit Seth's tea-colored eyes. Or anything else, for that matter. Like my father, Merton had been cut out of Seth's will. Neither brother had received a penny. A glimmer of truth dawned within me.

"Who's the nut case?" Victor wanted to know. But before I could answer, the ladder began to quiver. Victor scrambled to keep his feet on the top rung, clutching the lip of the eave in a death grip.

Was Kathryn shaking the ladder? She hardly seemed strong enough to manhandle a guy as big as Victor.

"You heard the lady," a wonderfully familiar voice shouted. "Get down here, Denton!"

Kyle! Kyle was shaking the ladder as if dislodging a coconut from a palm tree, forcing Victor to back down. Before he retreated, Victor stared at me one last time.

"It belongs to me, you know," he said.

"Why? Why should you have the pin?"

"Because my father didn't get a dime out of his old man. Seth owed it to him!"

"Then you are Merton's son," I declared. "Why didn't you tell us . . . Uncle Walker? He would have wanted to know."

"He doesn't give a damn about my father. Nobody does except me. After my mother left Dad, she married again and my stepfather adopted me. That's why my name is different. But I never forgot my father. He deserved something from this lousy family. The pin should be his!"

"Denton!" Kyle bellowed. "I'm warning you. Move or I'll yank this ladder away!"

I leaned forward as Victor began climbing down. "Where is your father? Where did Merton go?"

"Wouldn't you like to know?" was the only answer I got.

When Victor reached the ground, Kyle thrust him aside and hurried up the ladder. From my vantage point, I saw Victor flee to his car, which was parked behind some bushes near the driveway. He got in, gunned the engine and roared off with a flare of gravel.

Then Kyle was at the top of the ladder. "Holly, are you all right? That creep didn't hurt you, did he?"

I held out my arms to him. "Kyle, am I glad to see you! Just get me down!"

Both of us had a lot of explaining to do, and when my aunt and uncle returned early, obviously excited over something, there was only one thing to do: hold a council on the front porch with a pitcher of lemonade and a platter of Jinx's favorite cookies.

At first it was absolute chaos, with everyone clamoring to speak at once, until Kyle put two fingers to his mouth and gave a whistle shrill enough to make even Jinx retire to the banister, a pilfered Oreo in his beak.

"Shall we draw numbers?" Kyle suggested. "Apparently everybody has something important to say. Mr. Highsmith—this is your house, suppose you go first."

My uncle mopped his forehead with a handkerchief. "I can't believe what an astounding evening this has been. First we find my Rapunzel puppet in a pawnshop in Odessa, and then Alexandra confesses she knows Victor Denton stole it, and when we come home, because who can sit through a movie after that, we find our niece has been crawling around on the roof—"

"And she's found the missing pin," Zandra put in.

"Hold it," I interrupted. "What's this about finding Rapunzel?"

Aunt Gray took over. "We were walking down the street toward the movie theater, when Walker stops in front of a pawnshop with a cry. There right in the window is the marionette, big as life. We go inside and the owner tells us he got the puppet from a dark-haired young man who needed cash. And then Zandra says Victor stole it—"

"And it's my fault," my cousin moaned.

"How can it be your fault?" I asked her.

She poured herself another glass of lemonade. "A lot of things are my fault. Holly, I've been just terrible to you since you came. And for no reason. Until Victor appeared on the scene. Then I was jealous he liked you best."

I started to laugh. "If only we'd known—we were fighting over our cousin!"

"What cousin?" Walker wanted to know.

"Victor is Merton's son." I explained the complicated relationship, to their astonishment.

"I should have known it was something like that," Zandra said. "Victor wasn't really interested in me. I thought it was because of you, Holly. That's why I lied the night the puppet was stolen. I had unlocked that door to make Daddy think you did it. But when the puppet turned up missing, I was afraid Daddy would think I had something to do with it, so I lied."

"Did you suspect Victor?" Kyle asked.

"Sort of," Zandra said. "I tried to trap him into saying so that day in the coffee shop, but he was too slick." She sighed. "I wonder where he went?"

"Probably left town," I replied.

"I'm so ashamed," she admitted. "The things I did to get in Victor's good graces. I showed him the squint."

Now it was my turn to be confused. "The what?"

"It's a sort of a peephole used to spy on people," Walker said. "My father had one put in when he renovated the house. Lord knows why—I guess he thought it was amusing."

"Where is this . . . squint?" I asked, but I had an inkling.

"There's a passageway leading off the pantry, barely big enough to hold one person. There is a small hole cut into the wall between the passageway and my toy room, which used to be Seth's study." Walker turned on his daughter. "And you showed that to Victor? Why?"

She shrugged. "To bug you, mostly. I know how wild you are about your dumb old toys. After that time I took Victor into the toy room I showed him the squint. He thought it was great—he could watch what was going on in there and no one would ever know."

"I did," I spoke up. "I went in there a few times and I felt someone staring at me. It was eerie." Before Uncle Walker jumped all over me about going in his toy room, I added, "I only went in when the door was left open."

"Which seems to have been happening a lot lately," Uncle Walker said wryly.

Zandra raised a reluctant hand. "I'm the culprit, Daddy. I thought it was funny to use the key under the umbrella stand and unlock the door."

"But why?" he asked his daughter. "You know how valuable those toys are. Why would you do such a thing?"

I knew the answer to that one. Because Zandra craved attention and causing trouble was the only way she knew how to get it—the same reason she put the jester in my bed. She wanted to be noticed. At that time. But there was no need to go into that now. Zandra was clearly on the road to getting along with her parents. Let them discuss that in private. She flicked me a grateful glance when I said, "Doesn't anybody want to know how Victor got into the house?"

Naturally, they all did. I told them how I discovered the ivy ladder and the pane knocked out of the window. We all trooped around to see it, and I explained that Victor climbed the ivy, stuck his hand through the broken pane and unlatched the window. It opened outward just enough for him to squeeze through. He probably never even left the grounds the day he brought Zandra and me back from lunch, but hung around until we were all eating supper, then sneaked in and ripped off Rapunzel.

"But then he found out the pin might be valuable," Kyle said, "and decided to wait and see if it turned up before he stole anything else."

Back on the porch again, Walker said, "Let me see the brooch, Holly." I handed it to him, then unloaded my pockets. Jinx looked very interested in the pile of goodies.

"And it was in the crow's nest all the time," my uncle remarked, shaking his head wonderingly. He looked across the porch to where Kathryn sat on the glider next to Aunt Gray, her hands knotted in her lap. Throughout the explanations and confessions, she had said nothing. She met my uncle's eyes steadfastly.

"I think we owe Miss Fetzer an apology," Aunt Gray said gently. "She has been wrongly accused and has been living under that indictment for many years."

My uncle got to his feet and went over to Kathryn. "Please accept my apologies," he said humbly, extending his hand. "I've been as much to blame in this matter as my father. I hope you can forgive me."

Kathryn considered a few seconds, then took his hand. Her smile was as dazzling as the day she first enchanted my father, I was sure.

My heart swelled at my uncle's gallant gesture. It must have been hard for him to swallow his fierce Highsmith pride and admit his mistake, but he'd put Kathryn's feelings before his own. I admired him for that, realizing then that my mother was right—you *can't* choose your relatives. You have to accept them the way they are. I was glad to be a member of the Highsmith family, faults and all.

Uncle Walker gave the brooch back to me. "This is yours, Holly. You found it. It belongs to you. Alexandra told us in the car on the way to the movies how Victor thought it was a genuine Fabergé. If that's true, I imagine it's worth a pretty penny."

I regarded the enameled pin. One of the most famous jewelers in the world had made this, or a goldsmith under his direction. It was a slice of history and probably would command a high price if I chose to sell it. The money could help ease the financial strain at home—I could use it for college or to help Mom with the bills. And yet we'd managed all these years without a windfall. I guess we'd continue to do so.

The brooch didn't really belong to me.

For whatever reason my father left Kathryn, I felt obligated to make it up to her somehow. Daddy was a young man when he turned his back on Blackbird Keep—and since he never returned, he never *knew* Kathryn was still waiting, still hoping.

She had waited long enough.

Going over to Kathryn, I said haltingly, "My father—Artie—wanted you to have this." I laid the pearl-rimmed pin in her hand.

"Thank you," she whispered, clasping the pin to her heart.

When I turned around, Kyle was looking at me strangely, and I knew I had just had a Grand Moment.

I also knew many more were yet to come.

Delivered right to your door will be heart-felt romance novels by the finest authors in the field, including Diana Palmer, Brittany Young, Rita Rainville, and many others.

You will also get absolutely FREE, a copy of the Silhouette Books Newsletter with every shipment. Each lively issue is filled with news about upcoming books, interviews with your favorite authors, even their favorite recipes.

When you take advantage of this offer, you'll be sure not to miss a single one of the wonderful reading adventures only Silhouette Romance novels can provide.

To get your 4 FREE books, fill out and return the coupon today!

This offer not available in Canada.

Silhouette ❤ *Romance*®

Silhouette Books, 120 Brighton Rd., P.O. Box 5084, Clifton, NJ 07015-5084

**Clip and mail to: Silhouette Books,
120 Brighton Road, P.O. Box 5084,
Clifton, NJ 07015-5084**

YES. Please send me 4 Silhouette Romance novels FREE. Unless you hear from me after I receive them, send me six new Silhouette Romance novels to preview each month as soon as they are published. I understand you will bill me just $1.95 each (a total of $11.70) with no shipping, handling, or other charges of any kind. There is no minimum number of books that I must buy, and I can cancel at any time. The first 4 books are mine to keep.

BR28L6

Name	(please print)	

Address		Apt. #

City	State	Zip

Terms and prices subject to change. Not available in Canada.
SILHOUETTE ROMANCE is a service mark and registered trademark.
SilR-SUB-2

First Love from Silhouette

❦

DON'T MISS
THESE FOUR TITLES—
AVAILABLE
THIS MONTH . . .

SOMEONE ELSE Becky Stuart
A Kellogg and Carey Story

When Carey's New York neighbor vanished overnight, Kellogg and Theodore joined in the search. This led them to some unexpected conclusions.

ADRIENNE AND THE BLOB
Judith Enderle

What in the world was Adrienne going to do about the blob? Only Tuck thought he knew, and he wasn't about to tell.

BLACKBIRD KEEP
Candice Ransom

Holly knew at once that she never should have agreed to visit her uncle. His house was too spooky and its inhabitants even weirder. Would Kyle help her to unravel the mystery, or was he working against her?

DAUGHTER OF THE MOON
Lynn Carlock

From childhood, Mauveen had known that somehow she was "different." Should she listen to the ancient ancestral voices, or should she follow the promptings of her newly awakened heart?

WATCH FOR THESE TITLES FROM FIRST LOVE COMING NEXT MONTH

A DAY IN SEPTEMBER
Joyce Davies

"Seize the opportunity," Kim's horoscope had advised her. But first she knew that she had to put Kevin out of her mind and heart—at least that was the way it looked to her early that September morning.

A BROKEN BOW
Martha Humphreys

Dawn was haunted by her unknown heritage. Only Harry, her enigmatic neighbor, could help her, but could she believe the answers she read in his dark eyes?

THE WILD ONE
Tessa Kay

When Beth first glimpsed Con glowering by the cottage door, she knew she had found a modern Heathcliff. Did he recognize her as his Cathy?

ALL AT SEA
Miriam Morton

Casey loved the idea of working on an underwater project with Devlin. He was most definitely a deep-sea treasure! But first she had to fathom his negative attitude.

First Love from Silhouette